Charlie glanced back at Aimee, but she'd become engrossed in pushing a toy truck around the pit. Locking the gate-latch, Charlie spun around to join her father.

And froze.

The driver had climbed out of the car, cursing quietly as he surveyed the damage he'd caused. His American accent sliced into her.

"Marshall?" The name squeaked off her tongue as her heart stopped. *"Marshall?"* Louder this time but just as scratchy.

He turned in her direction and took away any lingering doubt as his intense green gaze locked with hers. In that instant she saw the man she'd shared a bed with for many wonderful hours. Her body remembered all the heat and passion, the sensual touches, and her deep, bottomless hunger for him.

Marshall Hunter.

The man she'd spent untold hours trying to find for their daughter had turned up outside her gate.

Dear Reader,

Taupo is one of those places from my childhood that I've never forgotten. We went there so my dad could go trout fishing. It was a much smaller town than nowadays; the houses were small, plain holiday homes, the footpaths unpaved, and no one was in a hurry. I have been back often for holidays, staying with my brother and his family, and seen Taupo grow into a busy, vibrant town. Despite the changes it is still the same wonderful place at the edge of a stunning lake and with a backdrop of mountains.

I chose Taupo for Charlie and Marshall's story as it seemed the perfect setting for a wounded hero trying to find his place in life. It's the antithesis to his constantly changing army life. It's where Charlie grew up, where she went to school, learned to sail on the lake, where her mother is buried, where her daughter was born.

Marshall has never lived in the same place for much longer than a year at a time. Charlie has never lived anywhere else than in the house that was her mother's family home. Does Charlie give this up to follow Marshall's erratic lifestyle? Or does Marshall take the plunge and learn to stay put in one place long enough to get to know it and the inhabitants well? Follow these two as they nudge their way towards the right solution for them both.

I'd love to hear from you at sue.mackay56@yahoo.com.

Or visit my place at www.suemackay.co.nz.

Cheers!

Sue

FROM DUTY TO DADDY
Sue MacKay

HARLEQUIN® MEDICAL ROMANCE™

Recycling programs
for this product may
not exist in your area.

ISBN-13: 978-0-373-06939-2

FROM DUTY TO DADDY

First North American Publication 2014

Copyright © 2014 by Sue MacKay

www.Harlequin.com

Printed in U.S.A.

Hannah, Phil and Austin—you rock.
Love you heaps.

CHAPTER ONE

CHARLIE LANG FOLDED her laptop shut and put it aside on the outdoor lounger she sat on, but continued to stare at the blasted thing as though it was to blame for all of her problems. Angst at her continued failure ate deep inside. 'I'm never going to find him, am I?'

Dad sat back on his haunches at the edge of the overgrown flowerbed he was weeding below where she sat. 'Aimee's father? Who knows, love? You've got so little to go on.'

Make that next to nothing. 'How many doctors are there in the US army called Marshall Hunter?' Her head spun with the frustration of it all, whizzing the ever-present fear into a maelstrom in the pit of her stomach. 'I must've sent hundreds of emails.'

'I take it the latest one bounced.'

'Yep.' Like every one before it. 'Why did he give me that address if he intended shutting it down?' Why had Marshall given her an address at all when he'd gone to great lengths to ensure she'd understood there couldn't be any contact between them after their fling finished?

On that last day, when he'd been heading back to war and she would shortly return to New Zealand, had he felt a sense of losing something special? She'd certainly been gripped by an awareness of impending loss. Had he suddenly found it impossible to walk away without some way of reaching her again? His note with the email address had been slipped into her shirt pocket while she'd been too busy kissing him goodbye and trying desperately not to cry. Trying to ignore the heat flaring through her body that one touch from Marshall had instantly triggered. Had always triggered—right from the get-go.

But he must've had another change of heart after he'd left Honolulu because not once had an email of hers got through to him. Fickle? Doubtful. Unsure of himself? Definitely not. Marshall had to be the most self-assured man she'd ever come across. Except when she'd asked about his family. Uncertainty had filtered into his steady green gaze then, only to be hurriedly blinked away and replaced with a cold, distant glare.

She'd understood instantly that to remain onside with him meant talk of his family was banned. Naturally, living with the outcome of that fling, she often wondered what he'd been hiding. Not that that was important right now. Only finding him was.

'Ever thought that the guy doesn't want to be found?' Dad never minced his words when he wanted to make a point.

'If I'm honest, it's blatantly obvious that's exactly what Marshall intended. In this day and age everyone puts their name, photo, even excruciatingly personal details out there in cyberspace so they can be found.' Everyone except Marshall Hunter. Which kind of told her what she'd been avoiding all along.

He really hadn't had any intention of ever having anything to do with her again—even in passing. That note had been an aberration she could put down to the emotional goodbye they'd been going through. Each kiss had been their last, only to be followed by another, and another, until Marshall's friend had hauled him away and into an army truck.

She'd stood, fingers pressing his kisses deep into her swollen lips, trying to keep Marshall's touch, his scent with her. Swallowing buckets of tears as the truck had disappeared round a corner, taking Marshall away forever.

Dad broke into her memories. 'Maybe you

should drop your search.' He'd been sceptical right from the start about the man who'd got his daughter pregnant. Fair enough, she supposed. Fathers expected every man coming within reach of their girls to treat them carefully.

But what Dad wouldn't concede was that Marshall didn't have a clue she'd had his child, wouldn't believe that Marshall was a good man at heart. Of course, Dad hadn't met him.

She knew different. Or so she told herself regularly. 'No, I refuse to contemplate that.' Marshall had affected her deeply the very first time she'd laid eyes on him in the ED at the hospital in Honolulu where she had been doing post-grad work. His intense gaze had locked with hers and they'd both stepped closer as he'd teased her about her accent. When he'd smiled at her she'd felt as though she'd found something, someone she'd been unwittingly looking for all her life.

At the end of their shift he'd taken her hand and led her out of the department, out of the hospital and along the road to the beach. Walking barefoot in the warm sand, the waves crashing only metres away, her hand firmly held by Marshall's much larger and stronger one and her shoulder brushing his arm, she'd thought she'd died and gone to heaven.

And in the warm air, with laughter and chatter spilling out from the restaurants dotting the foreshore, he'd taken her in his arms and kissed her so thoroughly her body had melted. She'd held onto him like he was a lifeline. Her body had wanted his, craved the release she'd known he, and only he, could bring her. Every nerve ending had desired his touch. Every muscle had trembled with anticipation.

Then he'd swung her up into his arms and run up the sand, across the road and into the first hotel they'd come to. She had always wondered what might've happened if a room hadn't been available. There'd been no way they could've made it all the way to the tawdry apartment block where the hospital provided rooms for temporary doctors before they gave in to the pulsing heat gripping them.

Their affair had started that night in a burst of passion that had been insatiable. It ended as abruptly two weeks later when Marshall had been sent away to some unknown place with his army troop.

She'd missed him ever since, as though he'd taken a chunk from her heart with him. Damn it. That hadn't been part of the deal. Neither had coming home pregnant.

'I wouldn't be looking for him if not for Aimee.' Yeah, sure. Her pride would've prevented her chasing after him like some lovelorn teenager. Did she love him? She'd enjoyed him and the things they'd got up to in bed. But love him? Unfortunately she had a feeling she did. Otherwise why else did she still dream of him most nights? What other reason was there for daydreaming about him moving here and sharing her home? Maybe marrying her?

Reaching for the laptop, she opened it and waited for her program to reboot. Reality sucked. And hurt. Her love wouldn't ever be returned, and yet it was vitally important she track him down. For Aimee's sake, at least. 'I always knew there was no future for us.'

Dad gave her one of his 'This is your father talking' looks that she'd known all her life. It would lead into something she should probably take note of. Except she was an adult now, didn't need her father's wisdom. Much.

'Why don't you stop trying to find this guy for a while? Save your energy for getting completely well again and then maybe it won't be essential for Aimee to have her dad here.' He tried to hide the quiver of fear colouring his voice but she knew him too well.

Staring at her dad, holding onto the surge of her own fear, she ground out, 'I have to find him. Aimee deserves a father, even if only a remote one.' Would Marshall be thrilled or furious when he finally learned her news? There was only one way to find out and so far that hadn't gone too well.

'You've put too much time and effort into this for most of the past year. Let it go for a while. Put it out there and see what comes back.'

'Dad? Put it out there?' Despite everything, a giggle spilled across her lips. 'Where did you get that idea?'

Dad's cheeks coloured. 'From your pal, Gemma.'

'That's typical of Gemma, but I never thought I'd hear you say it.' Gemma and Dad? Had she missed something? Gemma often dropped by on the pretext of seeing her and Aimee but what if her older friend's real interest was Dad? How did that make her feel? No blinding pangs of anger or disappointment struck. Surely that had to tell her something?

'Charlie,' Dad called loudly to get her attention back. 'What I'm saying is there are other things you could be doing with your time rather than getting obsessed about something you've got no control over.'

She sat back in the lounger and stared at the laptop screen. Her finger hovered over the pad, ready to open the internet link. Could she stop searching? For a while at least? Take a break from the heart-wrenching negativity that failure to find Marshall regularly dumped on her when she already had enough to deal with?

It wouldn't be easy when finding Marshall had dominated her thoughts for what seemed like for ever. This campaign had driven her to get up in the mornings when her body ached so badly she wanted to swallow pills and dive back into sleep to avoid the real world.

Doing what Dad had suggested might free her. Enable her to see the situation for what it was. She was a solo mother whose first priority was her daughter. Aimee needed her healthy and focused, not slumbering in self-pity and trying to do the impossible.

She closed down the laptop. Then she looked at her father, really looked, and saw the extra lines on his face, there because of her. Her chest swelled with love. 'Okay, Dad, here's the deal. I'll…' she emphasised her words by flicking her forefingers in the air '…put finding Marshall out there if you start focusing on getting your old life back. I don't mean working longer hours at the medical centre. I'm talking fishing, hiking in the mountains, meeting your pals for a round of golf.'

Pausing, she watched the longing flick through

his eyes so fast he probably thought he'd got away with it. She really had wrecked his life since coming home from Honolulu. Sticking her tongue in her cheek, she added, 'Did I mention dating? Definitely need to find time for that.' Should she bring Gemma's name into it? No, best leave that to Dad to sort out. For now anyway. She could give him a prod later if necessary.

'Dating?' he snorted. 'Me? At my age? You've been taking too many painkillers again.'

'Yeah, Dad, you. At your ripe old age of fifty-nine.' Thankfully right then a sound came from inside the house. Charlie usually heard her daughter crying almost before Aimee opened her mouth. Motherhood was so connected. As though a fine but strong strand of love ran between them so that deep inside she felt everything Aimee did.

'There goes my peace and quiet.' Charlie smiled, completely unfazed by the interruption.

Despite helping other women bring their babies into the world during her medical training, the overpowering strength of her love for one special little individual placed into her arms moments after the birth had been a revelation. And something Marshall had missed out on.

Her father chuckled as he returned to weeding the flowerbed beneath a pohutukawa tree.

Obviously not too fazed by the dating suggestion, then. 'Go on with you. You've been waiting for Aimee to wake up for the last hour.'

'True.' Driven by a sense of panic, of time running away on her and not knowing how long she'd be around for Aimee, she desperately wanted to grab every minute she could with her little girl. That same panic caused her to pause now. Was she forcing too much on Aimee? Rushing her through life instead of letting her learn to wait? To take each day, each little step slowly?

'You should let her cry for a bit.' Dad unwittingly underlined her thoughts. Sitting back on his haunches, he winked to take the edge off his comment. 'Never hurt you to wait for your mother to come and get you at that age.'

Charlie laughed, and deliberately refrained from standing up, even though she itched to do so. 'Maybe that's why I used to hate lying around in bed once I woke up.'

'Nah, that was because you were too active for your own good.'

'I got that from you. Aimee's the same. Guess it's in the Lang genes.' A yawn rolled up her throat and over her lips. It had been a long time since she'd been anything like too active. So long she'd forgotten how it felt to have abundant energy, not to need to go to bed till well after midnight.

When she'd finally gone back to work at the Taupo Family Medical Centre after her illness she'd truly believed she was ready for anything and everything, but her days off couldn't come round soon enough so she could catch up on sleep. Not easy to do around a toddler with the energy of a trailer load of Energiser batteries.

'Want me to get Aimee?' Worry tainted Dad's voice, adding to her sense of inadequacy. Not to mention her guilt for letting him see that yawn.

She tried for a grin, didn't do too bad a job. 'I'm making her wait, like you said.'

Dad grinned right back. 'Look at you. Almost bouncing in the seat with wanting to go pick her up.'

He did way too much for her. It broke her heart, knowing that when he'd decided to take early retirement so he could start having some fun she'd messed up his plans. Not that she'd asked him to cancel the big trip to Europe he'd looked forward to for years. But being the awesome father he was there'd been no question of what he'd do when they'd learned her dreadful news. He had stepped up for her all her life. More especially after Mum had died. And now he did the same for Aimee.

Would she be half the parent he was? Some days that worried her sick. On the really bleak ones it frightened her to think she mightn't get the chance to find out.

Aimee had evoked something primal within her. Like flicking a switch, bang, the love had turned on. Never to be turned off. A deep, unconditional love that had fine-tuned Charlie's protective instincts, while also bringing so much joy to her life. She couldn't wait for the years ahead to unfold. Already she watched with avarice as Aimee learned to feed herself, to stagger up onto her own feet and totter around the house, to give sticky hugs with those little arms—it all gave her so much pleasure. There'd be plenty more great things to come. She just knew it.

Wearing her Pollyanna hat? Definitely, though *she wasn't so naive as to think her daughter was going to be perfect*. Actually, perfection was a fault in itself. Not so long ago she'd believed her life couldn't get any better and look how that had blown up in her face. She was still recovering, might never return to the peaceful state of mind she'd innocently thought was hers for ever.

She shivered, rubbed her arms. Forced a smile. Pollyanna had quickly disappeared. The black worry that lurked at the edge of her mind expelled her happy moments all too quickly. Would that change one day? One day soon?

'Charlie?' Concern laced her dad's voice. 'You okay?'

With a lightness she didn't feel she replied, 'Sure am.'

Another cry from down the hall. This time Charlie didn't hesitate. Jumping up, she headed for the door. 'Yippee. Get up time. I want that first sleep-scented snuggle from Aimee.'

'Okay.' Dad conceded quickly enough. 'Now that my grandgirl's awake, I'll get the hedge trimmer out and tidy up out the back.'

Charlie paused, turned back. 'Dad, why don't you go play a round of golf instead? The hedge can wait another few days. Take a break from the chores and enjoy yourself.' Those lines around his mouth hadn't been there a year ago. They were all due to her. Guilt spread through her like wildfire. 'I'm so sorry.'

His face softened as he crossed to stomp up the steps to the deck, where he hugged her. His tone was gruff. 'Cut that out, Charlotte Lang. There's no point beating yourself up for something you had no say over.'

Sniffing in the dad scent she'd known her whole life, she blinked back tears and dredged up a smile. 'Have I told you that you're the best father ever?' The familiar line fell easily between them.

'Never.' That too was the usual response. 'Tomorrow, if the weather stays fine, I'll take the boat out on the lake with Billy to do a spot of fishing. How's that?'

That was progress. 'Great. I'll order up a perfect January day just for you. And I'll get the barbecue ready.' Of course the trout weren't so easy to catch in midsummer but the men would have fun trying. At least trolling meant a bigger chance of success than river fishing. And she'd get in steak as a back-up.

Yeah, she had a plan. Plans were good, kept her on track through the rough patches. Then it dawned on her to look around, see the day for what it was. The sun shone bright and hot in the clear blue sky, making everything appear brand new and the flowers on the pohutukawa sharp red. And her tiredness wasn't dominating her quite so much. In fact, she felt the best she had in a long time.

She surprised herself with, 'I'm going to start getting fit. Take my bike out of the shed and pump up the tyres.' She grinned, feeling the most relaxed she had for a long time. 'That will probably take all my energy and I'll have to have a nap afterwards, but it's a start.'

Until the advent of Aimee she'd loved nothing better than to fall out of bed and hit the road on her cycle before going into work. And on her days off most of her spare time had been spent sailing her Paper Tiger across Lake Taupo, catching the erratic winds.

'Don't overdo it,' said the doctor in her dad as he stepped away, averting his face in a vain attempt to hide his worry.

'As if.' Nowadays she took naps and spent her free time playing with dolls and building things out of plastic blocks with Aimee.

How drastically her life had changed since she'd returned home pregnant. She rubbed her tummy. Felt the surgical scar on her lower abdomen. Tried to ignore the flare of anguish. At least she'd had a child before her hysterectomy. She'd loved being pregnant and watching all the changes that had happened to her body. The months had flown past and then Aimee had arrived and she was in love.

Unfortunately, someone else had missed out on all that. Aimee's father. Marshall Hunter, US Army medic.

If only he'd been able to share in the excitement, to be around to put his hand against her expanding belly and feel his daughter kick. Even if she found him tomorrow, he'd never get any of that back. Aimee was eighteen months old and nothing like the tiny scrap of arms and legs placed against her breast moments after the birth.

How stupid of she and Marshall to agree to going their separate ways at the end of their fling. Despite her heart breaking, she'd gone along with him. He'd assured her he was single, that they weren't hurting anyone else, but he didn't do long-term relationships. Rightly or wrongly, she'd believed him. He'd come across as genuine. But no one had told her she'd have a child from that liaison. There'd been no thunderclaps to warn her she'd need Marshall Hunter back in her life nine months later.

Had Marshall flown to the moon? Even if he had, he'd still be contactable. Wouldn't he?

Well, she could be stubborn if it was important. And finding her daughter's father ranked at the top of the scale. But as of today she wasn't going to let the continual failure to achieve her goal get her down. She'd done with all that. It was time to start living full on, not half pie.

A louder shriek from down the hall told her Aimee was fed up with waiting. She wanted out of her cot—now. Being a determined little lady— wonder where that had come from?—she would quite likely attempt climbing out of her cot soon.

Charlie moved fast. A broken head would only add to the worries this little household already faced.

'Hey, beautiful, how's my girl? Have a good sleep?' Reaching for Aimee, Charlie's heart squeezed at the sight of the little creases made by the pillow on the side of her baby's face, and at the red cheeks and sleep-filled green eyes staring out at her over the edge of the cot. So like Aimee's father's eyes. Piercing green, reminding her of a polished emerald.

Aimee's father. MIA. She shuddered. Wrong term. She might be doing everything in her power to find him, but MIA? That was definitely tempting fate. Especially if he was back in another war zone with his unit. She touched the side of the cot with her fingers for luck, definitely needing to push away that cloud of dread.

'Mum-mum,' Aimee instantly gurgled, and raised her arms high. 'Mum-mum.'

Thoughts of Marshall kept trekking through Charlie's head as she lifted her daughter up. She couldn't really imagine anything happening to him. 'Your dad is so virile, so much larger than life, strong and full on. He looks the world in the eye, as though daring it to throw the worst at him.' He always acted as though nothing could touch him.

Stupid Charlie. Trying to get the man hurt now?

'Mum-mum.'

'Time you learnt a new word. How about Grandpa?' How about Daddy? If only there was a need for that.

Aimee wriggled and tightened her arms around Charlie's neck, almost choking her.

Carefully unravelling them, Charlie grinned. 'You've got a very wet bottom, my girl.' She kissed Aimee's brow and headed for the bathroom.

Blowing kisses on Aimee's tummy took up a few minutes. Giggles rent the air and made Charlie grin more widely. 'You're worth it all, my girl. I'd go through everything again if I had to.'

Careful, you might have to yet. No guarantees out there.

The dark thought lifted goose-bumps on her skin. It was this fear that kept her acting on the side of caution, kept her refusing to relax and accept she was over the worst so that she could get on with life, and that drove her to keep trying to find Marshall despite the unlikelihood of ever succeeding in that quest.

'Mum, up.' Aimee's well-aimed foot banged against her jaw, making her jerk back, and refocused her on where her mind should be. On her daughter.

'Hey, mischief, watch who you're kicking.' Yep, definitely an active kid.

Her baby girl, whom she'd do absolutely anything for. Along with Marshall's green gaze Aimee had inherited a whole dose of stubbornness from him. Otherwise she was her mum with the dark blonde hair, button nose and freckles dotting her cheeks.

'One day, my girl, we're going to find your dad. Won't he be surprised?' Surprise might not cut it. There was a myriad of other emotions Marshall would no doubt feel when he learned he was father to this gorgeous bundle of joy. Hopefully love would eventually come out on top.

But first she'd get her strength back. She sighed. Nothing was easy these days. Hadn't been since the day the lab results had come back with all the medical jargon screaming out at her: cervical cancer.

Charlie's world had instantly imploded. The future, in particular Aimee's future, had become a priority in case the worst happened and Aimee lost her mum. Fear had driven Charlie throughout her surgery and treatment, had got her back on her feet. Losing her mother to cancer at seven had been dreadful, but she'd had her dad to love and cherish her. If Aimee lost her to this terrible disease then she'd need Marshall in her life.

He was out there. He'd held her in his arms, made love to her a lot, kissed her senseless. He hadn't been an apparition.

Oh, no. Not at all. Her fingertips traced her lips. Her insides melted as her skin remembered his large hands caressing, teasing, loving her body.

Aimee needed to know both her parents. And…Charlie's fingers brushed the bathroom cabinet…if the worst came to the worst, Marshall had to be there for Aimee if she couldn't be.

If only she could find him.

She had to. No argument.

CHAPTER TWO

CAPTAIN MARSHALL HUNTER turned onto Spa Road and slowed, checking which side of the road he was driving on. 'Goddamned Kiwis. Why can't they use the right-hand side like everyone else?'

Someone tooted at him and he pulled to the kerb. 'Yeah, yeah, give me a break. I'm a tourist.' A tired smile stretched across his mouth. The trouble with being overtired was that everything got that much more complicated. Twisting the cap off the bottle of soda he'd purchased at the petrol station a little way back, he poured half the contents down his parched throat. At least that tasted the same as back home. Jet lag, and lack of sleep for the past six months, played havoc with his body. And his mind.

The military plane out of Kansas that he'd hitched a ride on had touched down at Whenuapai Air Force Base at the ungodly hour of five that morning.

Which only went to show how crazy he'd been. Why had he hopped a plane going in the opposite direction from Florida, where he'd intended spending some of his leave checking up on his buddy's family? A sudden aberration of the brain? Had to be. No other explanation for finding himself in this place called Taupo. On the long-haul flight, squashed amongst gear and guys, he'd tried not to dwell on his uncharacteristically impulsive action. Like that had been possible.

What had happened to Mr Cool, the guy who planned every move of his life? He didn't do random. Random got you shot in a war zone. Got you in all sorts of trouble anywhere. Besides, he was an officer in the army where lateral thinking didn't go down too well with the top brass.

Marshall grimaced. All control gone in a haze of yearning for something intangible, for someone who regularly flitted through his mind. So close yet so far away. Charlie Lang. Woman wonderful.

She'd been responsible for the fog in his head and the gnawing sense of finally reaching a destination he'd been aiming for ever since he'd waved her goodbye back in Honolulu more than two years back.

Closing his eyes, he leaned back against the headrest. Charlie. 'Because of you I've come all this way with no idea if I'm even welcome.' Of course he'd be welcome. Charlie would be thrilled to see him. Why wouldn't she? They'd got on well.

'You spent all your time together in bed.'

So? That had worked out just fine. Could be that they might do some more bed gymnastics while he was here. Unless she'd got hitched to some dude in the intervening years. Air caught in his lungs. She wouldn't have. Would she? Why not? Charlie was one very sexy lady who any man would be happy to get up close and personal with.

Okay. Don't go there. Presume until told otherwise that Charlotte was still single and willing. They *had* been very compatible. He'd never known sex like it. She'd pressed every button he had and some. One look at her across the ED and he'd been a goner, falling into those deep blue pools blinking out at him from under a thick blonde fringe.

His belly rumbled with hunger. Snatching up the BLT sandwich he'd picked up at the same time as the soda, he bit into it. Chewing thoughtfully, he hoped it was hunger and not nerves making his gut carry on like a washing machine. Like he ever did nervous. Not even on a recce when he knew armed insurgents were waiting to take a crack at him.

The sandwich went down a treat, making him feel almost human again. Ready to do battle. If it came to that. As if it would. Charlie would be happy to see him. But he'd been on edge for so long he couldn't quite get a grip on things. He'd come off that flight feeling like rubbish, knowing he should hop on the next plane out of the country, no matter where it went. But he hadn't. Instead, he'd gone looking for a way to get to Taupo.

A New Zealand officer at Whenuapai had organised a room on the base so he could scrub up, shave two days' growth off his face, change into civvies and have a decent meal. Then that same guy had driven him to the nearest car rental place.

Marshall knew he should've stopped overnight and caught some proper shut-eye. Instead, he'd been driving on foreign roads through a sprawling city, then through amazing countryside to reach this small town nestled on the edge of the country's largest lake. He might've been more prepared to cope with what he'd travelled so far for if he'd waited until tomorrow.

He snorted. 'For sure. If you're not ready to

see Charlie by now, know what you want to say to her, you're never going to be.' How else was he ever going to sleep properly again? 'But what am I going to say to her? Hey, buddy.' He looked up at the sky. 'Rod, you own this idea so help me out here.'

Sweat beaded on his forehead as his heart thudded against his ribs. Charlie was the woman he went to in his head at night after a hideous day on patrol. She was the woman who'd touched him like no other ever had. She'd gotten under his skin and wouldn't go away, no matter that he'd known he mustn't have her again. He had obligations that didn't include her. And yet here he was.

'It's not too late to turn around and head back up to Auckland.' But then he'd never have closure. Would always wonder what he might've gained by seeing Charlie one more time. This time he'd say goodbye properly so as his heart understood exactly where it stood. No notes slipped into her pocket.

Back in Honolulu he'd done the right thing by deliberately telling Charlie nothing about himself, not even which state he'd grown up in. He'd been strong, tough, thinking he was doing her a favour.

Their fling had been short, sweet, exciting

and hot, not to mention mind-numbing. At the end of it he'd hopped a plane ride out of Honolulu bound for the base in Kansas to prepare for his next posting to Afghanistan. He'd been so damned confident he could walk away from Charlie Lang without a care in the world, never to think of her again. Right? Wrong.

Glug, glug. The remaining soda coursed down his throat. Coming here had to be right up there with being totally selfish. But he didn't know any other way to exorcise Charlie from his brain, where she seemed to have branded him—with images of her gut-twisting smile, her light laughter, her very sexy body. Hell, even thinking about that turned him on. The heat south of his belt had nothing to do with his head and all to do with being closer to Charlie than he'd been in a very long time.

So he'd come to get her out of his system? Not to get back in the sack with her?

'Yeah, well, I'm a little confused right now.'

Not once in those passion-filled weeks had he asked where Charlie was headed after she'd finished her time in Honolulu. So sure had he been that he'd never follow up on her. But she'd told him anyway, making it scarily easy to locate her when he'd given in to the deepening need clawing at him. The world could be a very small place at times.

Now here he was at the bottom of that world, around the corner from Charlie's house. Soon he'd see her for real and realise his dreams had lied, that those wonderful memories were vapour, not real. That she'd been a very ordinary woman out for a bit of fun. Then he could get on with life the way he needed to live it, following his army career as hard as possible, even if it wasn't so rewarding any more. Especially as Rod hadn't made it. Guilt was his constant companion. Duty to his men his creed.

Voices washed over him as kids on bikes wheeled past the open window of his rental. Free as the birds they were. Sometimes he missed being a kid and being able to ride horseback around the ranch with his grandfather.

'Aren't you forgetting something?'

Yup. The weeks when Dad had come home on leave from the army and forced his discipline on his son. Harsh, unforgiving, relentless. That was the old man. He'd ruled by his fists. Hard to believe Granddad had spawned his father. Couldn't get two more dissimilar men.

Flick. His mind returned to the nagging questions that refused to die down. Would Charlie greet him with open arms?

Or would she give him a bollocking for breaking the pact they'd made in Hawaii?

Let's have fun and leave it at that. No contact afterwards, no regrets.

In the deep of the night when he couldn't sleep—most nights—he wondered if Charlie's willingness to go along with his ultimatum had meant there had been someone else in her life back here in New Zealand. Some guy she'd wanted to set up house and raise a family with. Had she been sowing some oats in Honolulu before coming back to marry? Whatever she'd been looking for at the time, he'd been a willing partner.

'Never going to know what she thinks while sitting here.'

Reaching for the ignition, he hesitated. Whatever it was deep inside his psyche that had brought him this far seemed to have suddenly deserted him.

Finally the engine turned over, purred loudly as though mocking this vacillation. He eased the vehicle back onto the road. His heart rate increased. Excited? Yeah, bring it on. He really wanted to see Charlie, no matter how she reacted. If she sent him packing he'd deal with it.

'At one hundred metres take the right-hand turn,' droned the GPS.

'Yes, sir.'

In Hill Road Marshall slowed, peered at letterboxes as he cruised along, finally finding Charlie's number. Lifting his foot from the accelerator, he glided the vehicle to the kerb and parked. Not stopping to overthink this any more than he already had, he pushed out of the clammy interior and leaned back against the hood, his arms crossed over his chest. He studied the house where Charlie supposedly lived. An old villa in good nick, surrounded by a recently cut lawn and weed-filled gardens, and with huge unusual trees equally spaced along the side fences.

Female laughter reached him, snuck under his skin, thawing the cold places deep inside. Charlie's laughter. He'd know it anywhere. It had warmed him, tickled and delighted him. Haunted him. Hungry for his first glimpse of the woman he'd flown halfway round the world to see, he scanned the veranda running across the front of the house. Movement from the side caught his eye.

A toddler, dressed all in pink, running and stumbling, shrieking with joy while waving a plastic bucket, heading straight for—for Charlie. Beautiful Charlie. There at last, right in his line of sight, was Charlie. In the flesh.

The air trickled from his lungs as he sank
further down onto the front of the car without shifting his gaze. An exploding landmine
couldn't have made him look away now. Memories of holding her close bombarded him, pum-
melling him with the sheer joy of her. Warmth
crept into his body. Had he done the right thing
coming here after all?

Charlie.

She seemed to still in her movements. Hell,
had he called her name out loud? Then she said
something to the little girl and jerked backwards
as she was rewarded with another ear-shattering
shriek of delight.

Marshall began breathing again.

And continued watching Charlie, recalling
how she'd race back to him after a long day
in the ED and leap into his arms, kissing him
senseless, before dragging him into bed. Not
that he'd been reluctant, far from it. But he had
enjoyed being seduced. It had been novel and
exciting. She'd teased him blatantly with her
body, but had always given what she'd promised. Then there had been the times she'd gone
all coy on him and he'd had to woo her into bed.

He ran his hands down his face and re-crossed
his arms. Was Charlie thinner now? Nah, probably not. His memory wouldn't be that accurate.

But her hair was very different. What had she done to those stunning long, honey-coloured tresses that he'd spent hours running his fingers through? Gone, replaced with a shorter, curly cut that framed her beautiful face. Different and yet equally attractive.

His heart slowed as he watched the woman of his nights reach down and lift the hyperactive bundle into her arms. Even from here he could see the love for the child all over Charlie's features.

Her daughter?

Pain slashed at Marshall. He was too late. Too damned late. Charlie was a mother. Which meant there'd be a man somewhere in the picture. She was taken. She hadn't changed the rules. Instead, she'd got on with life, made a family. That hollowed him out. Made him realise how much he'd been hoping she was free and available. Great. Now he knew, what did he do?

'You could just say hi.'

Sure. Now that he had admitted he'd been fooling himself all along, it hurt big time. His heart rolled over, cranked up enough energy to pump some much-needed oxygen around his body. Disappointment flared, mixed with the pain and despair, underlining the whole stupidity of coming here on a whim.

Getting reacquainted with Charlie again was not an option.

The reality struck, blinding him. He'd wanted to get to know her properly this time, to learn what made her tick. The doctor side of her, the serious Charlie, the loving, caring woman who enjoyed having a good time. All the Charlies that made up the woman who'd caught his attention when he hadn't been looking.

Another movement snagged his attention. Someone was walking towards the back of the house from under a big, bushy tree. Tall, thin, and, even from the back view, definitely male. Marshall's stomach dived. His arms tightened in on each other, holding himself together.

Damn it. He'd thought about worst-case scenarios and taken a punt anyway. But Charlie was now a mother and there was a man in her life. Marshall could no longer deny the obvious.

'You, Marshall Hunter, have to walk away. Now. Before she sees you and the trouble starts.' It would be so unfair to knock on her door and say, 'Hi, remember me?'

No way did he want to hurt her. And he surely would if he stayed now. Truthfully, he'd hoped for another fling, something he could walk away from. So now he'd have to suck it up and walk away sooner than he'd expected. Get on with life and put Charlie out of his head permanently.

But his boots remained stuck to the tarmac, going nowhere. He'd come too far just to walk away without a word.

'Oh, buddy, did you really think Charlie was sitting around, waiting for the day you might step back into her life?'

An image of her standing outside the hospital, blinking back tears and saying the sun was in her eyes as she'd waved him goodbye, slapped across his brain.

A little bit, he had. Okay, make that a big bit.

He needed to get over it. He'd had an absolutely sensational fling with her. One that he'd willingly walked away from with few qualms. And then she'd emailed. A month after Rod had been killed. Two days after he'd visited Rod's wife and kids and seen the anguish caused by Rod's passing. He'd deleted Charlie's message without reading it, knowing he never wanted to be responsible for causing her the same pain Karen suffered.

As Marshall watched Charlie and the little girl chasing around the lawn he thought of the hurt she'd been saved from by finding another man to share her life with. No doubt that man wouldn't miss birthdays and Christmas, would be around to fix the car when it broke down or to dig the garden, take her out to dinner. Things no woman would ever get from him. The army regularly sent him off to some hellhole in a bleak part of the world where he had to be strong for his men, not worrying about how he might be letting down the woman in his life.

'Time to go, buddy. You made a mistake coming here.' He blinked. Took one last, long look at the woman who'd unconsciously drawn him to Taupo, saw the things his memories hadn't been particularly clear on. The way she held her compact body as though ready to leap into his arms at any moment, except now it was her child she seemed ready to leap after. The gentle tilt of her head to the right as she concentrated on whatever the little girl was saying.

'Get the hell out of here,' he croaked around the blockage in his throat. Dropping back inside the car, he reached trembling fingers to the ignition. Blinked rapidly as the heat inside the car steamed up his eyes. Damn it to hell. He was too darned late.

CHAPTER THREE

CHARLIE HEARD A car moving slowly past the gate and glanced up. Not recognising the vehicle, she made to turn away but hesitated. Something about the driver's profile caught at a memory. What was it about that face that stirred her? Absolutely nothing. She bit down on the temptation to go out onto the street for a better look.

Losing her grip on reality now? Wishing Marshall Hunter back into her life wasn't actually going to bring him to her doorstep. No matter what Dad said.

Thump. Crack. The sound of metal crunching metal screeched through the air.

'What was that?' Charlie placed Aimee in the sandpit and raced for the gate.

'Sounds like someone wasn't looking where he was going.' Her father spoke from right behind her.

The car Charlie had noticed moments earlier was now parked with its nose deep into the side of their neighbour's SUV, the bonnet folded back on itself. 'John's not going to be too pleased about that. At least it doesn't look like anyone's been hurt.'

'Unless the driver had a medical event,' Dad pointed out as he strode past her. 'I'll go and check.'

Charlie glanced back at Aimee but she'd become engrossed in pushing a toy truck around the pit. Locking the gate latch, Charlie spun around to join her father. And froze.

The driver had climbed out of the car, cursing quietly as he surveyed the damage he'd caused. His American accent sliced into her.

'Marshall?' The name squeaked off her tongue as her heart slowed. 'Marshall?' Louder this time but just as scratchy.

He turned in her direction and took away any lingering doubt as his intense green gaze locked with hers. In that instant she saw the man she'd shared a bed with for so many wonderful hours. Her body remembered all the heat and passion, the sensual touches and her deep, bottomless hunger for him. Marshall Hunter. The man she'd spent untold hours trying to find for their daughter had turned up outside her gate. Just like that? No way.

Put it out there. Yeah, right, Dad.

The ability to stand upright deserted her. Her hand flailed through the summer air as she reached for the fence to hold onto, and her heart stopped. It must have because suddenly she couldn't breathe any more.

'Charlie.' Then he was there, directly in front of her, reaching for her, gripping her arms to hold her upright. 'How're you doing, babe?'

How am I doing? That's it? No *I came to see you.* No *Crikey what a long way from good old US of A to find you.* No *I'm just cruising through and thought I'd drop by.* Just how am I doing? Swallowing was impossible with the lump blocking off her airway. Her eyes widened as she stared at this smiling apparition with eyes that were deep green pools sucking her into an exciting world. An unrealistic world, she knew, but one she couldn't deny while so close to him. Her arms were heating where those strong hands gripped her. Her breasts seemed to be straining to be up close to that chest she'd once fallen asleep against in the wee hours of the morning.

'Charlie? I've surprised you.' Did he have to sound so pleased with himself?

'I'm fine,' she managed to croak out at last. Couldn't be better, in fact. Who did she think she was fooling? Not knowing whether to laugh or cry, she continued to stand there, stunned.

Then those wonderful arms she'd spent many hours longing for wrapped around her and tucked her against that expansive chest threatening to pop the seams of the black T-shirt he wore. That's when she knew this really was Marshall.

Something wet oozed down her cheek. Tears? She didn't do tears. Not once throughout her pregnancy when she wished Marshall by her side. Hardly ever during the harrowing days of waiting for the diagnosis of cancer. Hadn't cried while going through radiation and chemo. Must be the realisation that she didn't have to keep searching the phone records of every state in America to find numbers for every Hunter listed that was causing this leakage. 'You came,' she whispered.

'Were you expecting me?' As he leaned back at the waist to peer down at her, his mouth cracked a smile. A genuine, warm, toe-curling, Marshall smile.

And her heart went from slow to rapid in one beat. Heat rushed up her cheeks, dried her mouth so that when she spoke it sounded as though she'd sucked on helium. 'Don't be daft.'

'I'm daft now?' His smile widened, his eyes twinkled.

'I tried to find you. Except it seemed like you'd vanished into thin air. Even the army wouldn't help.' But what were the odds of Marshall turning up on her patch? Should she be buying a lottery ticket?

Marshall's arms fell away and he stepped back so fast she staggered. His tone was clipped. 'Of course not. They won't give out information on my whereabouts unless you're on my list of contacts.'

The temperature had suddenly dropped a few degrees. Of course she wouldn't be on that list. Hadn't expected to be, but Marshall voicing it reminded her how far apart they were, how little they'd had in common, or even knew about each other, except great sex.

And the sweetest little girl. Whoa. Red-flag warning. Her shoulders pulled back and her spine clicked straighter. She'd spent so much time trying to find Marshall that she'd never stopped to consider how she'd tell him about Aimee. Who knew what his reaction would be? What she wanted from him and what she might get could be poles apart.

Rubbing her arms, Charlie studied him. He looked exactly the same as the last time she'd seen him, the day she'd kissed him goodbye. Except then he'd worn army fatigues, not butt-hugging, thigh-accentuating jeans and a tee shirt that framed his size and muscles. His face was bronzed, his buzz-cut hair darker than midnight, that mouth that had done sensational things to her skin was still full and enticing. Marshall was still heart-stoppingly attractive.

Behind her someone cleared his throat. Dad. She'd forgotten all about him. Forgotten even where she was. And Aimee. Was she still in the sandpit? A quick look over the fence and Charlie relaxed a notch.

Aimee. Marshall's daughter. The tension rewound tighter than ever. And anger pounced. 'Why are you here? Turning up with no warning, as though you expected me to be happy to see you.' Her hands clenched and her breaths were short and sharp. After all this time of searching for him and here he was, looking wonderful, not to mention cocky. So darned sure of his welcome. 'Well, I don't want to see you.'

Her petulance rang in her ears. So much for being mature and sophisticated. Too bad. Right now Marshall bloody Hunter deserved worse.

Marshall was staring at her as though she'd

grown horns. She probably had. 'Charlie, I'm sorry. I never thought to phone ahead.'

She gaped at him, her jaw dropping hard. A fish out of water probably looked more attractive. 'You have no idea what you've done.' She spun round on the balls of her feet and nearly slammed into her father, who looked puzzled as he glanced from her to the man and back.

'Charlie, didn't I tell you to let it go and see what happened?' That Dad grin he gave her calmed her temper the tiniest bit. 'Happened a lot quicker than we expected, didn't it?'

He was taking the credit for Marshall's sudden appearance? No, Dad was being Dad, gentling her when her temper ran away on her. Thank goodness for fathers. On an uneven breath she said, 'You're right. I don't know what came over me.' Now, there was a fib. Marshall was no longer MIA but standing a metre away, watching her from those intense eyes that missed nothing.

Both men seemed to be waiting for her next move. She didn't have one. Her heart was thumping so loudly in her chest she couldn't hear herself think. Her stomach was doing loop the loop while her hands shook so hard she had to clench them into tight fists again.

Finally Dad made the first move. He strode

towards Marshall, holding his hand out in greeting. 'I'm Brendon Lang, Charlie's father.'

Marshall's eyes widened with something Charlie could've sworn was relief. Glad of the diversion? With startling alacrity he took Dad's hand and shook it. 'Marshall Hunter. Pleased to meet you, sir.'

Dad returned the handshake, said, 'Marshall, what happened? One moment you were parked on one side of the road, the next you've slammed into John's SUV on the opposite side.'

Embarrassment flushed through Marshall's eyes. 'I got distracted.' His gaze fell on Charlie. 'Forgot which side of the road to drive on. Do you know the owner of that vehicle? I'll need to sort out repairs with him.'

'John's our neighbour. I'm surprised he's not out here already.' Dad glanced up the drive.

'He went out on his motorbike hours ago.' She'd growled when John had roared down the road moments after Aimee had finally fallen asleep.

Dad crossed to the merged vehicles. 'Let's see what the damage is.'

Marshall looked embarrassed as he called after him, 'I'll shift the rental and then leave the guy my contact details. He's not going to be too pleased when he sees that dent.' He didn't move to join Dad, instead remaining beside her, playing havoc with her senses. He was an eye-ful, for sure.

Tightening her stomach muscles in an attempt to gain some control over her wacky emotions, she looked up at him, and instantly wished she hadn't as her eyes clashed with his. A girl could get lost in those eyes. Heavens, she once had. And look where that had got her. Focus on the bent cars. Nothing else.

'I think you'll survive. It's John's work ve-hicle, supplied by his company. If you'd hit his Harley you'd be swinging from that tree in his front yard already.' The words spilled out in a rush.

Marshall grinned that mesmerising grin she'd never forgotten. 'Really? A Harley? Awesome.'

Great. Another motorbike freak. And some-thing she hadn't known about him. Along with just about everything, she realised. A doctor in the US army didn't cover much about this man at all. Hang on, don't forget his energy, athleticism and how gorgeous he looked first thing in the morning with stubble darkening his strong jaw.

A shiver rocked through her. Stop it. None of that had anything to do with Marshall sud-denly turning up unannounced. Why now? She shrugged. Plenty of time to find out. Or was there? He could be passing through. Of course, Waiouru. The military base was only a few hours down the road. This would be a fleeting visit. She'd have to make the most of it and grab the opportunity to tell him about Aimee. But why was he here? Then reality hit—hard. 'You were driving away. You weren't stopping by to see me at all.' What had he been planning on? A reunion? Changed his mind when he'd seen how suburban she actually was?

'Caught.' His smile faded as his lips pressed into a line. His gaze drifted to Dad, back to her. 'Sorry, Charlie. I decided I'd made a mistake.'

'Marshall.' She grabbed his forearm, shook him to get his undivided attention. When those eyes that reminded her of hazy summer days met hers this time she all but yelled at him, 'Don't think you're disappearing out of my life that quickly. Not when I've spent months try-ing to trace you.'

There was no way she'd let him walk away now. Her gut rolled, which had absolutely noth-ing to do with Aimee and everything to do with the wickedly hot memories of Honolulu that touching his arm brought to mind.

'You have?' Shock dropped his jaw. 'Why?'

Gulp. Not out here on the street. The man

deserved some lead in before she dropped her bombshell. She shrugged, trying for nonchalance and failing miserably. 'If we sort out the vehicles first, will you promise to give me a few minutes of your time?' A few minutes? She'd better come up with a succinct explanation for why she'd been searching for him if that was all the time available.

'Yeah, sure.' Marshall's tone lightened as though he thought he'd been granted a reprieve.

As if. How could he know that? He was very astute, remember? Said it was part of his military training to always be looking for a hidden agenda. What he hadn't worked out yet was that it would be a very short reprieve. But first the cars. 'Think you'll be able to back your car away from the SUV without causing more damage?'

Then he leaned closer, traced a fingertip over her lips. 'How have you been, Charlie? Really?'

Her stomach thrummed. Her lips opened under his finger. Just like that, she was his. Or would be if she wasn't standing in the street with Dad watching warily. Jerking her head back, she glared up at him, saw the man who was used to getting what he wanted when he wanted it, and started to spew out two years' worth of desperation. 'I couldn't be better, what with—'

Aimee interrupted, 'Mum-mum. Up.'

Charlie spun around to find Aimee half-draped over the fence. 'You little monkey. That fence is supposed to keep you in.' Seemed she'd be arranging for the new, higher fence to be built sooner than she'd expected. Opening the gate, she bent to lift Aimee into her arms. 'Come here.'

Her heart was pounding as her blood sped around her veins. She'd nearly blown it then, had been about to spill it all thoughtlessly, without due consideration for Marshall and his reaction. That would definitely not earn her any points and make it harder for Aimee in the long run.

'Your daughter?' Marshall stood right behind her.

'Yes.' She saw disappointment cloud his eyes. So he didn't like the idea she had a child. Didn't that fit in with his plans? Whatever those were. Tough. She had more bad news for him yet. When he heard the whole story he wouldn't even be thinking about how he felt about *her*.

Charlie held Aimee tightly against her chest. A shield? Did she need protection from Marshall? Now the moment of truth had arrived she suddenly wondered how he might react to being told he was a father. He might go absolutely ballistic and deny flat out he could ever be a father. Or say there was no way in hell he wanted a part in Aimee's life. Or he might insist they move to the States to be near him. Not a hope in Hades, Marshall. Not a hope.

'Go sort out your car, Marshall.' Now she sounded bossy. But what was she supposed to do? Tell him everything here and now, standing on the footpath? Hand him Aimee and say, 'Meet your daughter'? 'Will you stay long enough for a coffee afterwards?'

Marshall's eyes widened. Struggling to keep up with her? 'Sure.' He turned towards the vehicles, turned back. 'It's great to see you, Charlie. Really great.'

Take my breath away, why don't you?

Her eyes feasted on his broad back and narrow hips as he walked away. A shiver of excitement rippled through her. But there was so much she didn't know about Marshall. Once she'd tipped his world upside down with the news he was a father, would she get the chance to find out anything? Or would he storm off, never to be seen again?

Her gaze drifted to the entangled vehicles. He wouldn't be storming anywhere in the next few minutes. Her spirits lifted. He had to hang around for a bit. At least until a new car had been arranged, surely?

Marshall headed for his rental, still trying to collect his scattered brain cells. This tall dude was Charlie's father. Hell, he'd nearly shouted with laughter when he'd heard that. All the disappointment gripping him since he'd spied the guy under the tree had dissipated in a flash.

You're not in the clear yet, buddy. That cute little girl has to have a father. Kids don't just arrive in the letterbox.

His smile slipped. True.

'Right, let's get this sorted,' Brendon muttered, just as a Harley shot around the corner.

'This your neighbour?' He tilted his head in the direction of the bike. What a way to introduce himself to Charlie's father. If the man had any sense he'd make sure he never went near his daughter again.

'Yes. Come and meet John.' Brendon seemed preoccupied. 'Are you staying in town, son?'

Straightening his shoulders, Marshall studied the man before him. There seemed to be a lot more to that question than was apparent. Until he got a grasp on the situation he'd give away little about his intentions. Intentions? Hell, they were as clear as a sandstorm. 'Yes, sir.'

'For long?'

So the guy did want him gone. Wasn't happy about his sudden appearance. Protecting his daughter? 'Two days. Maybe three, depends on my ride out of the country.'

'So you're flexible?' Was that hope lightening that steady gaze? Nothing made much sense here.

'Depends on the air force.' Not to mention Charlie and her situation. 'I'd like to spend some time catching up with your daughter, if that's at all possible.'

'You'd better stay the night with us, then.'

I don't think so. In the circumstances that's way too close and personal. 'Won't Charlie object?' What about the kid's dad?

Brendon gave him a knowing smile. 'Probably, but then she'll calm down and see the merit in my idea. You might have to weather her temper first, though.'

'Seems like I've already had a wee dose.' Marshall shook his head. He'd never once seen her get angry back in Honolulu. 'Let's talk to your neighbour about his wrecked SUV first.' And give me time to decide whether I go for broke or head for a hotel in town.

Stay in the same house as Charlie? And not be able to touch her, or to hold her, kiss her like he ached to do? Because if he did he was sure he'd be history. It would go down a treat with her old man. The guy seemed decent enough but touch his daughter and there'd be hell to pay. Marshall just knew it.

Then he was being introduced to John and they got down to the nitty-gritty of sorting out his bad steering problem.

Charlie stood at the window, peering through the trees. Spying on the men. Pinching herself. That really was Marshall out there. With Dad. Talking as though they'd always known each other. There didn't seem to be any animosity from Dad, just his regular caution.

She grinned despite the tension gripping her. Dad must've just about wet himself when she'd spoken Marshall's name. For all his saying to leave it up to the universe to sort her problem, he would never actually have thought anything would come of it. She'd better remember to tell Gemma. She'd enjoy a good laugh.

But Gemma could wait. The man the universe had delivered to her doorstep was about to take all her attention. Strange that now he was here she felt reticent about telling him about Aimee.

Once Marshall knew he was a father Aimee was no longer hers alone. Someone else would have the right to make decisions about her life. Talk about selfish. She definitely wasn't being fair to Aimee or Marshall. There again, if Marshall wasn't interested in being a hands-on father, nothing would have changed. Except that if her health turned to custard, Aimee would still have a parent to go to. Marshall would have to take her then.

But it had been one thing wanting to find him with the intention of explaining the whole situation. It was a completely different issue to actually front up to him and turn his day upside down, if not his life.

More than two years ago he'd been adamant he didn't wanted commitments and she was about to ask him for the biggest one possible. Part of her felt sorry for the guy. If only she'd probed a little to learn what lay behind his statement. But every time she'd started to ask serious questions he'd leaned in and touched her, with the resulting heat turning her brain to molten desire. By the time they'd made love she'd forgotten everything else.

'Mummy.' Aimee tugged at the hem of Charlie's shorts. 'Want dink.'

'You want a drink,' Charlie enunciated clearly

for her little miss. Hard to believe how quickly
Aimee was learning to talk. Almost overnight
she'd gone from saying nothing to these funny
little sentences. Aimee was a gift. A joy. She
had to get that message across to her daughter's
father so he wouldn't miss out on anything else
as Aimee grew up.

Male laughter filtered through the trees.
Seemed everyone was getting on just fine. No
surprise there, with John being so easygoing
and Dad acting as middle man. Marshall could
also charm anyone when he put his mind to it.

Including her. Not that he'd had to try very
hard. She'd been his in a blink. Never before
had she known such excitement with a man.
Marshall had truly shown her past lovers to be
beginners. He'd known all the buttons to push
or caress or kiss, turning her into a sex addict
overnight. A Marshall sex addict. There had
not been even a hint of anything sexual since.

Trying to ignore the old but familiar sweet
tension in her tummy, she turned away and
headed for the kitchen and the juice, tidying
away toys as she went. Aimee tended to spread
everything far and wide when she was playing, making it a constant job to keep the floor
clear enough to get from one room to another.
Normally just thinking about it made Charlie

feel tired but not today. Right now she felt more invigorated than she'd felt since she'd first become ill.

Must be something in the air, she hummed to herself. Or a certain American on her doorstep. Her lips twitched. Marshall Hunter was here. In Taupo. Outside her home. Unbelievable. And then the tears really started, pouring down her cheeks, dripping off her chin.

Brendon told Marshall to go on inside the house, and that he'd be along shortly. Marshall could feel his antennae twitching. It was as though Brendon was pushing him and Charlie together—for a catch-up chat? Or was there more to it? But no one had known he'd turn up this afternoon so that couldn't be right.

Did Charlie mind him being here? Or was she about to kick him to the moon? He couldn't decide if she'd truly been happy to see him or not. Initially she'd all but thrown herself at him, but only moments later she'd pulled back, hard.

He stepped into the warm interior and paused to suck in a breath. It had been a long haul to get here, no point in retreating now. Until today he'd never retreated—unless his life had been in danger. Or his buddy's.

His mouth soured. Now was not the time to

be recalling that bleak day in hell. Fronting up to Charlie could never be as painful as dealing with what had happened to Rod. The man after whom he'd promised to name his first son, if and when he ever got around to settling down and raising kids. Some time around when he reached fifty.

Stepping along the wide hallway, he glanced at the framed black-and-white photos on the walls. Most of them featured Lake Taupo with the mountains in the background. They were very good. 'C Lang' was signed across the bottom-right corner. Charlie did photography? Darn, he knew so little about her.

He found her in the kitchen with the child. Definitely thinner than he remembered. Had pregnancy done that to her? Most women put on weight, didn't lose it. Could she have taken getting back into shape too seriously? An image of running along the beach in Honolulu with Charlie at his side sprang up and he smiled. Yes, Charlie had been a fitness fanatic. Had loved her sports almost more than anything else. Almost. Sex had been top of the pops. But that was a kind of sport too, she'd told him one day, a cheeky grin lighting up her face.

'What did John have to say?' the woman in question asked in a strained voice as she kept her back to him and supervised the little girl drinking juice. Most of the liquid made it into the child's mouth but the pink tee shirt had a yellow streak down the front.

The pranged cars. Of course. Focus, man. 'He seemed okay with it all.' Marshall tried for a nonchalant shrug to hide these oddball emotions charging around his head. He needn't have worried because Charlie continued focusing her attention elsewhere. He told her, 'I've phoned the rental company and they'll sort it out, including supplying me with another car.' His eyes were stuck on the child. She was so cute. Except for the eyes, she had her mother's colouring right down to the freckles on her button nose.

'Bet they loved that,' Charlie sniffed, and he knew she was crying.

Three long strides and he stood in front of her, reaching his fingers to trace the wet lines on her face. 'Hey, babe, don't cry. Sorry if I've upset you by turning up out of the blue. If you want me to disappear, I'll go. Pronto.'

Panic flared, widened those damp eyes that flicked from him to the child and back again. 'You can't go. Not yet.' She hiccupped through her tears and swiped at her face again.

Why the panic? Then he was holding her, wrapping his arms around those thin shoulders and tucking her up close to his big, warm body. Protecting her. From what? Himself? Hell, he hadn't even thought about taking her in his arms. It had just happened. And Charlie hadn't slapped him across the face and pulled away. He liked holding her. Liked feeling her small frame against his larger one, even if there was a frailty to her that hadn't been there before.

'Charlie?'

'Yes?' came the muffled reply against his chest.

'Why are you shaking?' Tremors had begun rocking through her. 'Why the tears?'

She said nothing.

Placing his hands on her waist, he tipped back a little to put some space between them. Hell, she was thin, bony even. Was she all right? 'Talk to me. Please. Tell me about you. About your daughter.'

Charlie's face whitened, and again panic flared in those haunting eyes. She nodded. 'Yes. Of course.'

What was going on here? Didn't she want him asking about her family? That seemed odd. What about her partner? Only one way to find out. 'You married now?'

Her head swung from side to side, that distinct unease still all over her demeanour. 'No. What about you?'

She wasn't going to change the subject that easily. 'Is this your house?'

'We share it with Dad. I grew up here. I do have a house in town, which I bought a couple of years ago, but it's rented out at the moment. Dad helps with looking after Aimee.' She drew a long breath and opened her mouth, and another torrent of words spilled out. 'We both work at a medical centre—'

Marshall placed a finger on her lips, felt an electric sizzle up his arm. 'Slow down, Charlie.' Under his hands the trembling continued. Because of him? Did his touch disturb her? Or was she afraid of something? He dropped his arms to his sides and stepped back, putting space between them. 'Are you all right?' he asked again. She'd better be. He couldn't bear it if something bad had happened to her.

Her chin ducked abruptly. 'I'm fine.' Then, 'I'm still getting over the shock of seeing you outside our house. Why were you driving away?'

Because I'm a prize idiot. 'Don't get the wrong idea here.' I'm not a stalker. 'I'd been parked outside for a few minutes, watching you and wondering if you'd welcome me or not. Then I saw your father walking around to the back of the house and got the wrong idea.'

'So you drove away.'

'I didn't want to give you any problems. We had an agreement back in Honolulu and obviously I've broken that.' Had to. Had needed to get over her by seeing her again. But already doubts were creeping in under his skin. Would he ever be able to get over Charlie?

'So if you hadn't gone all American and driven on the wrong side of the road, I'd never have known you were here?' Anger laced her tone and those eyes fired up. 'You'd have gone away without a word?' she hissed, leaning closer.

'I thought I was doing the right thing by you.' Now *he* was on the back foot. What had just happened?

Her forefinger jabbed his chest. 'Do you have any idea how hard I've tried to find you?' Jab. 'Agreement or not?' Jab. 'I have spent…' jab '…untold hours on the computer, searching for you.' Jab. 'And you were driving away.' Then her anger disappeared as quickly as it had risen. Her chest rose and fell fast. 'Sorry. It's just that I wanted to find you and now you're here and I don't know how to tell you something important.'

Warning bells started blaring in his skull.

Nothing Charlie said made any sense and yet he was on high alert. Incoming attack. Stepping back further, he leaned one shoulder against the wall and crossed his ankles, to all appearances totally at ease. But inside his head he was pulling up every scenario imaginable. Because something big was about to go down. Something very big.

Then Charlie glanced from him to the little girl. A sob broke across her lips.

And shocked realisation slammed into him. The green eyes should've warned him.

'Aimee's mine.'

CHAPTER FOUR

ALL THE AIR in Charlie's lungs whooshed out.
Her arms instantly wrapped around her waist.
And she stared, like her eyes were glued to Marshall's stunned face, watching and searching.
His gaze, firmly fixed on Aimee, showed nothing of his thoughts. Not a hint.

Her heart crashed repeatedly against her ribs
as fear and hope warred in her brain. Would he
walk? Would he stay? At least stop long enough
to hear the rest? Would he shout at her? Call her
all sorts of names for not telling him, even when
she'd tried so hard to get in touch? Or blame
her for getting pregnant in the first place? The
skin on her arms lifted in chilly bumps. Why
had she not prepared for this moment? Yeah,
right. Like how?

'Mum, mum.'

Charlie reluctantly dragged her eyes from
Marshall and checked out her daughter. Their
daughter. Oh, hell. Her stomach clenched. She

clamped her hand over her mouth as nausea rose. This was so—so big. So difficult. Swallow. Swallow.

'Charlie? It's true, isn't it? I'm a father.' Those beautiful green eyes shifted their focus to her. Questions fired out at her.

Another swallow and she answered his first one. 'Yes.' The word whispered across her bottom lip. She swallowed, tried again. 'Yes, Aimee is your daughter. She…' Then the words locked into a lump at the back of her throat, refusing to budge.

'Holy Toledo.'

That was a good response. Wasn't it? It didn't sound bad. At least he was acting calm. So far. She managed, 'She was born a little over eight months after I got back from Honolulu.'

'You didn't have any way of contacting me.' A ton of regret darkened those words but no blame. Then, 'So this is why you've been trying to find me.'

'Yes.' He didn't need to know the rest yet. 'It's a lot to take in.'

'Where do I start?' He sounded completely bewildered. His bemused gaze flicked back and forth between Aimee and her.

At least he wanted to start. But wait until the shock completely wore off. It might be a differ-

ent story then. Charlie turned to Aimee, who
had her cup upside down, pointing in the general direction of her open mouth. Aimee. The
love of her life. The reason she was in this situation. Warmth sneaked into Charlie. She never
got tired of watching her daughter.

'Up, up.' Aimee's face began screwing up for
an outburst.

Moving quickly, Charlie reached for a damp
cloth to wipe some of the mess off Aimee's face
before lifting her to hold her tightly. She wanted
to hand Aimee to Marshall but for the life of
her she couldn't. She froze, unable to make
the move. Unable to share her daughter with
this man. Their daughter, remember? Looking
over the top of Aimee's head, her gaze clashed
with Marshall's intent one. Was this when he
ran screaming from the house, never to be seen
again? Admittedly he'd handled himself well so
far but it had only been a few minutes since the
truth had dawned on him.

His face softened from shock to awe. 'Charlie Lang, a mother. It suits you.' Then his gaze
shifted infinitesimally, slowly cruised over
Aimee. Looking for?

She said, 'She's got your eyes.'

'Yeah.'

'You want to hold her?'

His hands jammed into his pockets as he took a backward step.

Okay. Too soon. Shuffling sideways with her heavy bundle, she flicked the kettle on. 'I'll make that coffee I promised. How do you take it?' Her stomach would probably heave if she drank any but she had to do something other than hold Aimee, who'd gone very quiet and still. Twisting her neck, she saw Aimee studying the man in their kitchen.

'Black and strong.' Marshall was suddenly avoiding looking at either of them, apparently finding the view out the window far more interesting.

Aimee wriggled to be put down. Placing her carefully on her feet, Charlie watched as she tottered over to Marshall and stood staring up at this stranger. An important stranger, if all went well. Rubbing her hands up and down her arms, she wondered what to do if Marshall decided he didn't want anything to do with Aimee. Even if her health didn't let her down, every child was entitled to two parents.

The need to explain things gripped Charlie and she began talking fast. 'From the moment I found out I was pregnant I wanted you to have the opportunity to decide what role you'd have in your child's life.'

He turned back to face her, saying absolutely nothing. Thankfully his steady gaze didn't condemn her.

So she continued. 'I've spent a lot of time looking for you in between having Aimee and learning to be a good mum. I checked every known social network on the net. Then I started phoning M Hunters in various states.'

His eyes widened as he gave a grim smile. 'Truly?'

'You wouldn't believe how many there are in the US.' Too many. Her phone bills were horrendous some months. 'Marshall, I don't want anything from you. Not for me. Certainly nothing like money or other handouts. Because of an inheritance from my mother I'm comfortably off and can easily provide whatever my child needs as she grows up. But I do want you to know her. Aimee needs her father to be in her life in some capacity.' Her mouth was getting drier by the word, her tongue beginning to stick to the roof of her mouth.

Marshall's steady gaze unsettled her. What was going on in that head of his? If only he'd say something. Like what? *I'm thrilled to learn I've got a child. Let's play happy families and see how that goes. We know nothing about each other but our child will solve all the differences.*

Sounding good so far? Absolutely wonderful. If it wasn't completely fictitious.

Marshall watched the emotions scudding across Charlie's fragile-looking face as she babbled at him. He could read her like a neon sign. She was filled with the need to explain, to be fair and honest, and yet she was afraid he was going to skew everything for her and her little girl. That really stung despite knowing she was right on that score. But not in the way she imagined. She knew nothing about him. Had no idea he would make the worst father imaginable because of the upbringing he'd had. His fingers zipped across his head. What if he'd inherited his father's genes? No way was he going to find out. The stakes were too high for all of them.

Clearing his throat, he hurried to put her at ease. 'Charlie, whatever happens, however I decide to play this…' Play was the wrong word. He shrugged, temporarily out of the right words, then carried on. 'I will never try to take Aimee away from you. By that I mean I won't demand she lives with me six months of the year or anything equally hideous.'

She didn't relax. 'You would have a fight on your hands if you did.'

'I figured.' He tried for a smile, managed to

paste something resembling one on his face. 'You could've picked a far better guy to be Aimee's dad.' If only he was more like his grandfather than his own father. A caring, tentative farmer, not a hard-nosed soldier and disciplinarian.

Her beautiful eyes widened. 'Come on. If I believed that I wouldn't have bothered looking for you.' Then she added with a hint of the fun-loving Charlie he'd once known, 'You're a wonderful man. Any girl would be proud to show you off on school sports day.'

'Sports day?' Gulp. 'You're years ahead of me, Charlie.' He was still trying to grapple with the fact he'd spawned this little kid currently shoving building blocks through juice in the middle of the floor. Kind of messy. Kind of cute. Slam. His heart squeezed. Hard. *She's mine? I did that? Helped make Aimee?* He dragged his knuckles down his cheeks, digging in deep, checking he was awake, if he was feeling something or this was a dream. Everything was real. All too damned real. Spinning around, he charged for the door. He needed air, needed to get out of Charlie's space. Needed to think without seeing Charlie's concerns glittering out from those tragic eyes.

Why did she look like that? He didn't remember seeing anything but laughter in her eyes and face before. Guess last time had been all about fun. Today was about consequences and reality.

Stumbling down the front steps, he charged down the path, reining in the urge to run faster than he'd ever run before. This situation was not going to go away. Looking along the road, he saw the crunched-up vehicle he'd driven down from Auckland. What a mess. Right now New Zealand didn't seem to be agreeing with him.

Spinning around, he strode away in the opposite direction, trying to outwalk what he'd left at Charlie's house. But she followed, in his head, as did that little cutie named Aimee. They were probably never going to leave him again. Even when he was on the other side of the world, fighting battles, looking out for his comrades, those two females would be lurking in some corner of his mind. Gulp.

Since when did he let situations get the better of him? He was trained to face adversity and deal with it. Despite the sense of free-falling from a plane without a parachute, he grinned. Or was it a grimace? In the army they didn't teach you to deal with being told about eighteen-month-old daughters.

But you're more than a soldier. You're a doctor. Doctors nurtured, cared, mended, saved.

Hadn't saved Rod.

He swore. Loud and badly. Stared up at the sky. 'What do you think about this, then, *buddy*? Huh? What the hell am I supposed to do now? Quit soldiering? Move down under to a tourist town with a big lake and a small population? Be a father?'

'Hey, watch out, mister,' a young voice yelled.

Marshall dropped his head, glared around. Hell, that had been close. 'Sorry, kid, didn't mean to do that,' he called after the boy on a bike. A horn tooted from behind him and he nearly leapt out of his skin. He had to get a grip. Standing in the middle of the road, shouting up at the heavens, was going to get him killed. Or locked up.

Waving an apology at the car's irate driver, he stepped off the road onto the grass verge that led down to the lake edge. Sinking down on his haunches, he studied the terrain. The choppy water didn't stop kids leaping and diving into the chilly depths. Beyond them sailboats and motorboats sped back and forth. On the shore-line scantily clad people laughed and chattered under sun umbrellas as they tried to cool off. All very innocuous. Summer fun, family time.

Two things he'd had next to none of, and then only with his grandparents. A rare wave of anger swept over him. He had missed out on things other kids took for granted. His parents had never taken him out for the day just to have fun. He sucked up the anger, swallowed it. Thought about Grampy and Granny. They'd had more than enough love to spare for the skinny kid who'd arrived on their doorstep every school break.

They'd been his mentors, and yet he lived by his father's role model. Always on the move, never stopping one place long enough to make friends or have a relationship that lasted longer than a couple of weeks. He'd met his only close friend in officer training camp and they'd been in the same unit ever since. Yeah, and look where that had gotten the guy. In a wooden box far too soon.

The same thing could happen to him any time. Active duty meant danger and the very real danger didn't take note of who was in the firing line. Rod had been one of the best and he'd still bought the big one.

Shuddering, Marshall asked himself how he could be a good father for Aimee. He'd be in and out of her life, never stopping long enough to go to that sports day Charlie had mentioned. It would be better if he told Charlie right from the get-go that she should find a decent man and settle down to raise Aimee properly, lovingly, knowing from day to day, week to week, that he'd always be coming home. Because she sure wasn't going to get that from him.

In the laundry directly off the kitchen Charlie mechanically folded clean washing and sorted it into piles. Where had Marshall charged off to? More importantly, was he coming back? Her heart slowed. That might've been the last time she'd ever see him. The only time Aimee saw her father, and unfortunately her wee girl had no idea who Marshall was to her.

But Marshall took responsibility very seriously. She'd seen that first hand while working with him in Honolulu. It wasn't something he switched on and off in different situations. It was as intrinsic to him as breathing. The only time she'd met his friend, Rod, in Honolulu he'd told her Marshall put looking out for his men before everything else, including his own safety.

Marshall hadn't said Aimee had nothing to do with him. When he'd declared, 'Aimee's mine,' without a doubt in his voice, the world had stopped moving. Round one to Marshall. Except there were plenty more hurdles to come. None of them would be easy. They had a long way to go towards making this shared parenthood work. If he came back.

He would. Her fingers reached for the table-top, brushed the wooden surface lightly. Please.

Dad walked into the kitchen. 'Think it's probably about time for a cold beer. Wouldn't you agree, Marshall?'

'Can't say no to that,' came the deep rumble of the voice she'd been straining to hear for the last hour.

She sighed and dredged up a smile. This putting it out there seemed to work. Marshall had returned. Now the fireworks could start. Or maybe they wouldn't. She'd try to give him the time and space to absorb the startling news he'd never expected to hear.

'Hey.' A shadow fell across her.

Her tummy squeezed with longing when she looked up into the eyes that had been a part of her dreams for so long. Hunger flared for that fun they'd shared, for the uncomplicated nights when they'd explored each other's bodies, the simple pleasure of walking hand in hand along the beach to watch the sunset. Even a need tugged at her for that professional camaraderie when Marshall had mentored the intern fresh from medical school. But none of that had a place in this situation. 'Hey to you, too.'

'Sorry I charged off. I went down to the lake while everything sank in.' He looked genuinely contrite. 'I hope you didn't think I was running away.'

She winced, went for the truth. 'I hoped you hadn't, but I did wonder if you'd disappeared from my life again.' Even she heard the sadness in her voice. 'It must've been a huge shock.'

His forefinger traced her bottom lip. 'One I hadn't prepared for, that's for sure. But I'm back and you have my undivided attention for the next day or two.'

'I can go with that.' More than she'd expected, less than she'd hoped for. She placed the neatly folded towel she'd been gripping against her chest on the pile in the basket and stood before Marshall, studying him. Butterflies spread their wings in her stomach, fluttering wildly as she noted the well-honed muscles of his upper arms.

She'd missed him. Two weeks of wild passion and she'd spent the intervening years thinking and dreaming about him, wondering how he was, where he'd gone, who he might be with. And now he stood before her, looking superb in his casual attire.

Leaning forward, she stretched up onto her toes and reached for his mouth with hers. When her lips touched his all those long months of yearning disappeared in a haze of heat. It was as though they'd never gone their separate ways, as if the intervening time had been a figment of her imagination. Her hands slid around his neck, pulled him closer so she could deepen her kiss and press her tongue to his mouth to slide it inside.

And then Marshall was hauling her up against his hard body, his hands splayed across her back as he held her to him. His lips claimed her mouth with a hunger that surprised and shocked her. Marshall had missed her, too. His tongue danced around hers. Her body melted into his, trying to become one with him.

She forgot everything except Marshall. His arms holding her, each one of his fingers pressing into her skin under her T-shirt like hot brands, his hard thighs that reached as high as her hips, that taut belly against her soft baby tummy. His hardening reaction to her.

'I'll take the beers outside to the veranda.'

Her father's quiet voice pierced her euphoria, returned her to normal quicker than anything else could've done. 'Thanks, Dad,' she managed to gasp.

Surprise radiated out of Marshall's eyes. 'Sorry. I got carried away. What will Brendon think of me?' Embarrassment coloured his cheeks as he let her gently down onto her feet then adjusted his jeans.

'He's pleased that you've made my day by turning up. He'll give you some slack.' Still reeling from the abrupt end to that electric kiss, Charlie raised a wobbly smile. She'd acted rashly, but Marshall did that to her.

'Your father knew about me?' His fingers rubbed at his eyelids.

A bubble of laughter rolled up her throat. 'It was only this morning Dad suggested I give up searching for a while, concentrate on—on other things. So I sort of agreed, and here you are. If I'd known you were going to turn up I'd have saved myself hours of trawling through web sites.'

'So Brendon's not going to send me on my way just yet?'

Dad would never do that unless he thought Marshall was bad for her and Aimee. 'Not a chance. Now, let's go and be social with him and get that beer into you.' Pulling the fridge door wide, she found some lemonade to fill a glass. After adding a squeeze of lemon juice, she led the way outside. 'Come and sit in the shade for a bit. Dad will crank up the barbecue soon and we'll cook you a Kiwi dinner.'

* * *

Marshall followed Charlie through the large villa, glancing into rooms they passed. The lounge room was enormous and tastefully decorated. The furniture was stylish yet comfortable. Everything appeared well maintained. Bet that took some doing in an old house like this one.

Stepping onto the veranda, he took the bottle of beer Brendon held out to him. 'Thanks.' At least there was no animosity in the other man's eyes. Certainly some curiosity. He supposed any father would want to check out the guy his daughter had taken a fancy to. God. How embarrassing to be caught necking only hours after catching up with Charlie.

'Take the weight off your legs.' Brendon indicated a chair.

Even though he'd have preferred to stand, having spent hours squashed up in the plane and then behind the steering-wheel of the car he'd wrecked, he did as he was told. No point in getting any further offside with the guy than he might already be, despite those friendly eyes. Charlie pulled up another chair beside his and plonked her cute butt down, careful not to spill her drink. He asked, 'You're not drinking wine these days?'

'Not since I found out I was pregnant.' Her

glance was distant, as though he'd touched on something important. Like what? It had seemed an innocuous question. But how would he know? There was so much to learn about Charlie. Now that there was a child in the picture he couldn't walk away. So much for getting Charlie out of his system with a brief visit. If nothing else, Aimee had put paid to that theory. Fooling himself again. He wanted much more of Charlie, and Aimee.

He dug for another, maybe safer topic to chat about. 'This place is huge. You must rattle around inside. Or do you take in boarders?'

'Not likely, despite having five bedrooms and two lounges.' Charlie smiled over her glass, those aqua eyes bewitching him with their twinkle. 'Plenty of space for when we've had enough of each other.'

Brendon sat, stretched his legs out to the edge of the veranda. 'It's one of the original homesteads built more than ninety years ago. It belonged to Charlie's mother's family.'

Charlie added, 'Mum was born here. Then I was born here.'

'And now Aimee.' He looked around. Where was the little girl? His daughter. Holy Toledo. His daughter. His chest expanded with pride, even though he hadn't had anything to do with Aimee up until now.

'No.' Charlie chuckled. He'd forgotten how often she'd do that and how it had warmed his heart each time. 'Aimee was born down the road at the maternity hospital. I definitely didn't want a home birth.' She leaned forward and pointed under the trees. 'She's in the sandpit. Her favourite place at the moment. Long may that last.'

'Keeps her occupied while you get things done?'

'You've got it. I'm dreading the day she thinks tree-climbing is the best thing to do. There's a hut in that tree by the fence that I used to spend hours in.'

'She fell out and broke her arm once.' Brendon grinned. 'That's what's bothering her about Aimee getting big enough to climb up there.'

He shuddered. 'I don't blame her. They're mighty tall trees. What are they?' His neck clicked as he tipped his head back to stare up at the odd trees.

'They're native fauna. That one's a rimu.' Charlie pointed to the one where the sandpit was. 'The flowering one is a pohutukawa and the big one in the far corner is a kauri. The wrong varieties to grow in town but every time

Dad talks about cutting them down I get upset. It takes for ever to grow a kauri so big.'

'They must've been planted way back when this house was built by Charlie's great-grandfather. The land surrounding the house has been subdivided off over the years,' Brendon told him.

For the life of him Marshall could not imagine living in the same house his great-grandparents had. It was inconceivable. Even Grampy had only owned his farm for twenty years, and while it had been the one place on earth Marshall had hated to leave at the end of school holidays he still couldn't imagine living there week in, week out for years at a time. He shook his head.

'Charlie, haven't you ever wanted to move some place else? What about you, Brendon? I'm presuming you moved in when you married Charlie's mom.'

Two similar faces with the same piercing blue eyes stared back at him, amusement widening their generous mouths. 'Why would I?' they answered almost in unison.

'But there's a whole world out there.' He spread his hands, careful not to spill beer over the decking. 'Different homes, towns, people.'

'But this is home. Taupo is my birthplace.

It's where I went to school, learned to sail, met my best friends, where Mum's buried. This is where I want Aimee to grow up. She might not stay but I hope she'll come back from time to time.' Charlie looked bewildered. A cute frown formed between carefully styled eyebrows.

Alien. That's what her concept was. Totally alien. He leaned back in the chair and tipped the beer down his throat. Kiwi beer. Icy cold and tasty. Yeah, he could get to like this. Except he wasn't hanging around long enough to get used to anything.

Charlie was still watching him. 'Where did you grow up?'

'Everywhere and nowhere. I was an army brat, with two career soldiers for parents.' The next mouthful of beer soured on his tongue. It all sounded quite crappy compared to Charlie's life. But that's just how his life had been. Still was and probably always would be.

Look at this visit. Two days, maybe three in New Zealand before he flew back to the States and on to who knew where. Wherever his men went he went, making sure they were safe, or at least doing everything possible to keep them that way.

'That's terrible. I can't begin to imagine what that must've been like.' Her sweet mouth turned down, as though she was hurting for him, or the unhappy little boy he'd been.

Because she'd have guessed he had been unhappy. Not that he'd ever have admitted it, not back then, not now. But he'd known he'd been missing out on things, especially friendships, which was why he'd worked hard at being Mr Popularity at every school he'd attended. Trying to make the most of things all the time. 'I got to see plenty of new places.'

When the hurt entered her eyes he knew he'd been flippant. Had probably meant to be but equally he really didn't want to upset her. Charlie deserved better from him. 'It wasn't much fun,' he told her. 'But there was one constant in my life back then and that was school holidays with my grandparents. They took me in and gave me some stability until I was twelve.' Until the accident that had changed him for ever. Having to watch Granny suffer as they'd waited for help to arrive had set him on the path to becoming a doctor.

A childish shriek came from the direction of the sandpit and Charlie was up and off the veranda double quick. 'Hey, sweetheart.' She bent down at the edge of the pit and scooped Aimee up, plastering kisses over the scrunched-up little face. 'What's wrong? Did you drive the truck over your toes again?'

Aimee shook her head slowly from side to side and shoved a thumb in her mouth.

Gently removing the thumb to kiss it, Charlie peered down into the sand. 'Did Teddy fall off the truck?'

Aimee's head changed direction as she nodded agreement. Her gaze moved from her mother to Brendon. Then on to him. Those same eyes he had, as Granny had had. The moment they'd registered in his brain he'd known she was his. Not the tiniest of doubts. And while the reality had slammed through him he hadn't wanted to deny it. A strange sense of hope, of gladness, had taken over and spun him out.

Since when had he thought he wanted a child in his life? Never had, never should. This strange reaction had to be because his body clock was all out of whack after the long flight down here. But what if he could be a good dad? Not that it was likely with his pedigree.

Marshall's breath stalled in his throat. Those young eyes remained locked on him. He couldn't break the contact. Could Aimee read his mind? As if. She didn't yet grasp the concept of what a father was or did. Hell, he didn't want to disabuse her of any ideas Charlie might teach her about that, but he'd have to tell her the truth about his background one day soon.

Panic flared his nostrils, dried his mouth so that he had to pour some beer into it. But his bottle was empty.

'Here.' Brendon handed him another; icy cold and slick with condensation. 'Get that into you.' There was understanding in the man's eyes, in his voice.

'Thanks,' he croaked.

'Give yourself time.'

Didn't the guy get it? Did Charlie? He glanced in her direction, found her gaze fixed on him, too. Hell, everyone seemed to be keeping an eye on him, waiting for something from him. They weren't going to be happy. Despite learning about his appalling childhood of being hauled half across the country and back every year, they honestly thought he could do this. Could be a rock-solid father for Aimee. Damnation. He already had a whole troop of men to take care of.

Look at the three Langs. Completely at ease with their lifestyle and each other. Charlie and her father had a strong, loving connection that must've got them through a lot over the years, and would continue to do so long after he'd returned to duty. He didn't have that with either of his parents. He and Charlie? Chalk and cheese? Try the earth and the moon. That's how far apart they were, how different their lives were. They didn't have a hope in Hades of making this work.

CHAPTER FIVE

THE NEXT MORNING Charlie dressed with more care than she'd bothered with in forever. Zipping up her denim shorts, she muttered under her breath. She needed a belt to keep them up. Not fair. They'd fitted perfectly back when she'd first bought them at the market in Honolulu. Back before her treatment regime had burnt off all her body fat and then some.

Rummaging through the wardrobe, she found a near-new sleeveless blouse made in a soft cotton fabric and slipped it on. The bright reds and blues added some colour around her pale face. Not even spending time in the sun every day had tanned her skin to a healthy bronze this year. Would she ever look robust again? Would her strength come back if she worked out hard enough? She needed energy before she could work out. Even now, ten months after her last radiation treatment, there were days when walking to the letterbox was exhausting.

Her mouth twisted into a wry smile. Last night, when she'd announced she was off to bed at nine o'clock, Marshall had looked nearly as shocked as when he'd cottoned on to Aimee being his.

'You're what?' he'd blustered.

'Being a mum and a doctor wears me out,' she'd explained, once again avoiding the real issue.

Now, slipping into Aimee's room, she found the cot empty. She glanced at her watch to make sure she hadn't slept in. No, she'd got that right. Guess Dad had got up earlier than usual to get ready for his fishing trip.

No sound came from the kitchen but the front door was open so she headed in that direction, pulling up short the moment her feet hit the veranda. No way. She had to be hallucinating.

Marshall lay sprawled on the lawn while Aimee crawled over him, giggling when he tickled her. Marshall's total absorption in this simple game made her heart squeeze. This was what she wanted for her daughter. A father who played with her, who would take the time to do things for her and with her. There was wonder in Marshall's gaze, as though he couldn't believe he'd created this gorgeous tot.

Had he never thought about having a family

of his own? From the little he'd mentioned yesterday about his childhood it probably wasn't at the top of his to-do list. Her heart squeezed painfully. She'd always thought she'd have children some time in her future. Children, as in more than one. It hurt to think that dream was over. Being grateful for having Aimee didn't always cut it. Her daughter would never have siblings. *She'd* never again feel a baby growing inside her body. It was damned hard to swallow at times.

Marshall looked up then and smiled that easy smile of his. 'Hey, you're looking good.' His gaze trawled over her.

'Thanks.' She blushed.

'Mum, mum. Play.' Aimee delivered a soft punch to Marshall's chin.

'Hey, small fry, watch it.' Marshall grinned and lifted Aimee up into the air above his head, rocking her gently as she shrieked with laughter.

The man was a natural. Aimee had obviously fallen for him already, appearing totally relaxed in his grasp. She'd definitely have made it known if she had any qualms. That had to be good.

'I hope it was okay to get Aimee up. She was chattering away to herself when I got up thinking about going for a run, so I figured I'd bring her out here and let you snooze a bit longer. Last night you looked so tired I thought you'd fall asleep on your feet.'

Charlie sat down on the steps. 'I was a bit zonked. Must've been the excitement of you turning up.'

'I'm losing my touch if you want to go to sleep when I'm around.' His smile turned into a grin, and set her heart racing wildly.

Her cheeks burned crimson as his gaze intensified, firing up memories of what they used to do in the evenings after work. She'd certainly never fallen asleep until the wee hours of the morning. 'Guess I'm out of practice,' she murmured.

'Really?' His grin stretched. 'I like that.'

'You're a bit cocky this morning.' She grinned back. Obviously he'd slept well. Sadly, not even Marshall's presence in her home had kept her awake for more than a few minutes last night. Sleep came far too easily these days. As for long, hot nights with Marshall, she doubted she'd last more than half an hour before nodding off.

A shiver ran up her back. A familiar pang of fear snatched at her previously happy mood. The uncertainty of her future seemed far worse now that Marshall was back in her life. He might be going away again but now that he'd met Aimee he'd keep in touch. He had to. Selfishly, that made her wish for more. She'd wanted to make contact for Aimee's sake, but now she knew she'd been lying to herself. She'd never got over him, had compared every man she'd dated since—all two of them—to him and had found them lacking in just about everything. Those two weeks had a lot to answer for, and not just her precious little girl.

'Charlie?' Marshall stood over her, Aimee in his arms. 'You okay? You've gone pale.'

I was pale before. 'Something stepped on my grave.' Ouch. She sucked a breath through clamped teeth. Wrong thing to say. There wouldn't be a grave for many years to come. Funny how she'd started to accept she just might make it, yet now with Marshall here on her patch the doubts and fears were creeping back in. Even more to lose than before? Did she want a future that had Marshall in it? Apart from as Aimee's dad?

Pushing up off the step, she reached to kiss Aimee on the cheek. 'Good morning, sweetheart.' And when Marshall leaned closer she rose onto her toes and kissed his cheek too. Except he moved and her lips found his. *Good morning, sweetheart.*

'Good morning, beautiful,' Marshall murmured against her mouth. 'You are a sight for sore eyes.'

'Mummy, hungry.'

Reluctantly pulling her lips away from that sensational mouth, she looked at her daughter. 'Hungry, eh?' Flicking Marshall a look, she asked, 'Have you been teaching her new words?'

He grinned. 'I tried for "Can I have lots of kisses?" but so far "hungry" is it.' Aimee wriggled to get down. Marshall obliged, carefully placing her on her feet, before straightening and draping an arm over Charlie's shoulders. 'Want me to cook breakfast? I do a mean piece of toast.'

Slapping her forehead with the palm of her hand, she groaned, 'How can I resist?'

'Morning, everyone.' Dad strolled out onto the veranda dressed in his lucky fishing trousers. Bending down, he plonked a noisy kiss on Aimee's forehead. 'Hello, poppet.'

'Hungry.'

'Well, that's a good thing because I'm about to cook up a storm. A bloke needs a hearty meal before he heads out on the lake to catch the family dinner.' Dad looked from her to Marshall. 'Ever been trout fishing, lad?'

'No. Tried salmon fishing in Canada once. Had a great time but didn't catch a thing.'

'I'll take you out some time. If you come back this way.' Talk about a loaded statement.

Charlie held her breath but Marshall shrugged it away with absolute ease. 'Sure. Want a hand with that breakfast?'

A totally noncommittal reply. She swallowed her disappointment. It was better this way than having him make promises he wouldn't keep once he'd had time to really think everything through.

'Can always use another pair of hands.' Dad seemed to accept Marshall's non-answer, and if anyone would be pushing him that would be Dad. This whole situation was unsettling for him too, worrying if she might pack up and head for the States so she and Aimee could be near Marshall. But Dad needn't worry. She wouldn't be doing that.

She smiled as she watched the men walk down the hall to the kitchen, Aimee tottering along behind. Amazing that Dad and Marshall appeared totally at ease with each other. Was Dad trying too hard to make Marshall feel welcome? She hoped not. She wanted Marshall to make up his own mind about what he was going to do. Anyway, he had an army career to get back to. A career that was unlikely to bring him anywhere near New Zealand.

Her heart sank. So much for being excited about having him around. This really was silly. She'd needed Marshall to know about Aimee, and now he did. The last thing even she expected was for him to give up his career. He might be a doctor but first and foremost he was a soldier. That had been abundantly clear in Honolulu when the call had come for him to report back to base earlier than originally expected. He'd immediately gone to the head of the ED and told the guy he was leaving. No asking if that suited, or could the department cope with being left in the lurch. The army and his men came first. And, she suspected, second and third.

'You're missing out on your run,' she muttered as she headed for the cupboards to get plates down.

'I'll go later. Maybe tomorrow you can come with me?'

Ouch. Once upon a time there had hardly been a morning she hadn't gone for a run or cycle first thing. 'I don't run any more.' The plates hit the bench with a bang.

'You don't?' Astonishment cracked through the air. 'Why not?'

'I had to stop in the last months of pregnancy and I've never got back to it.' Please don't ask any more.

'Charlie.' She felt his hand on her shoulder, turning her to face him. 'Am I missing something here?'

'I...' Swallow. 'You know what? I will go with you tomorrow but you'll have to go easy on me. Not try and race me home, as you always used to.' Hadn't she decided to start getting fit yesterday? No time like now to start. Hefting the plates, she headed for the door.

Marshall's eyes narrowed as she tried to pass him. He opened his mouth and she waited for the questions. But they never came. Slowly he leaned forward and kissed her lips lightly. 'It's a date.'

Marshall didn't know what Charlie was hiding from him but, sensing her unease, he'd let it drop. For now. He didn't have the right to interrogate her. Not until he'd spent more time with her. But tomorrow they'd go for a run and see if that didn't open up a line of conversation that might shed some light on the matter. Judging by Charlie's lack of strength, it would be a very short run. Had something gone horribly wrong during her pregnancy?

In the meantime, he'd concentrate on her father. He found it hard to make Brendon out. The guy made every effort to be friendly yet surely he had plenty of questions ready to fire at him. Taking the bacon and eggs the older man handed him, he said, 'I'll do my best to do what's right for Charlie and Aimee. I can promise you that.'

What I can't promise is not to hurt them. I know little about being a parent. Also, I will never ask Charlie to tie herself to me for the rest of her life. That would be a half-life. I'd hardly ever be around.

'I'm sure you will.'

That's it? The guy was playing with him. Had to be. 'You know nothing about me.' Neither did Charlie, come to that.

Brendon banged a pan on an element. 'You're right. I don't, but I trust Charlie's judgement.'

'That's it?' he repeated out loud. 'Come on. I can see you've got questions begging for answers. Fire away.' He pulled his back ramrod-straight, tightened his shoulders and faced the man down. At least he tried to but Brendon wasn't intimidated at all.

Shaking his head, Brendon asked, 'How do you like your eggs?'

Anger sped through his veins. What was this

man about? Trying to scare him off in a weird, roundabout way? 'Charlie mentioned you'd suggested she give up looking for me. Would you prefer it if I hadn't got in touch at all?' Except not once, even when Brendon had seen them kissing, had this man indicated he had problems with his sudden appearance.

Crack. The fat sizzled as an egg slid into the pan. 'I've watched my daughter spend months trying to find you, only to be disappointed every day she failed. It was very important to her you know about Aimee. Now you do. So, no, lad, I am happy you've turned up.' Crack, another egg hit the fat. 'Can you throw some bread in the toaster? We'll eat outside on the veranda. The cutlery is in that top drawer.'

If Brendon had been thinking clearly he'd have remembered who had dried and put away the cutlery last night after their barbecue. Something was rattling him, something Marshall desperately wanted to know. But he couldn't offend Charlie's father by persisting with his questions. 'What does Aimee eat?'

'Toast and honey.' Brendon's stance relaxed.

Charlie breezed into the kitchen, her earlier unease gone. 'I could kill for a cup of tea. What about you, Marshall?' Switching on the kettle, she leaned back against the bench and folded her arms under her luscious breasts.

'Make that coffee and I'm in.' Trying to avoid staring, he turned to study the toaster, waiting for the toast to pop up. A hard-on now might change Brendon's attitude towards him. But his mind had other ideas, bringing up memories of what was under that bright blouse, of his hands holding her breasts, his thumbs rubbing the nipples until Charlie cried out with need.

The smoke alarm shrilled at the same time his phone vibrated in his back pocket. Black smoke streamed up from the toast he was supposedly watching. He jerked the plug from the wall and tipped the burnt bread into the sink, all the while listening to Charlie and Brendon going on about the American who couldn't even manage to cook a piece of toast.

Brendon reached for the 'off' button on the alarm, a smile lightening his face. 'Remind me not to ask you to cook anything again. Or drive a car.'

'Your dad is hopeless, sweetheart.' Charlie lifted Aimee into her arms, grinning like a cat that had just had a bowl of cream.

Dropping more bread into the toaster, he grinned back. 'Hopeless, am I?' Leaning over, he brushed a kiss over her lips. 'We'll see about that,' he whispered.

Blushing, she spun away. 'Didn't you just get a text?'

His grin faded as he read the message. 'Seems my flight's leaving early. Tonight at eight and I have to be at Whenuapai by seven. Damn.' He texted a reply and shoved the phone deep into his pocket. 'I'd better pick up that replacement rental car after breakfast.'

Charlie's face tightened as she turned away to make their drinks. Guess she hadn't wanted him leaving yet. They'd barely got past the Aimee disclosure and he was leaving. No doubt she had many things to tell him. Plenty more kisses to share? And no time. 'Why don't we walk into town later to get it? Take Aimee with us?' And talk as we go.

'Sounds like a plan,' she mumbled.

He started another lot of toast, this time keeping his eyes focused on it.

'Another scorcher of a day,' Marshall said as he pushed Aimee's stroller along the footpath.

'Hope Dad remembers his sun block. The number of times he's come home off the lake redder than a strawberry is unbelievable, considering he's a family doctor supposed to be warning his patients about the dangers of melanoma.'

'Did you become a doctor because your father was one?'

The things Marshall didn't know about her. 'In some ways I guess I did. I liked the way he helped people and could make them better. The community spirit of general practice also appealed. But I honestly can't remember a time I wasn't going to do medicine. At ten I thought surgeons were the best then at twelve I liked the idea of radiology. Pathology followed until Dad pointed out how isolated pathologists could be.'

'I can't quite see you sitting behind a microscope all day.'

'No, I'm definitely more of a people person and being a GP suits me, though I toyed with the idea of specialising in emergency medicine right up until I found out I was pregnant.'

'Did that have anything to do with your time in Honolulu?'

'You can wipe that cheeky grin off your face.' She playfully whacked his biceps and wished she could wrap her hand around it. 'Yes, you made the ED exciting for me.' When his grin stretched further she shook her head at him. 'Not the after-hours stuff back in our rooms but the nitty-gritty urgency of traumatised patients. I liked not knowing what was coming through the door in the next moment. I loved being tested again and again. It was stimulating.'

'So why change your mind because you were pregnant?'

'I wanted to have my baby in Taupo and there isn't a big hospital with a major emergency department here. Also, being a solo parent didn't faze me but I preferred to be near Dad. He brought me up on his own. I wanted him to be a part of Aimee's growing up.' Please leave it at that.

Of course he didn't. 'I looked this place up and saw that there's a major hospital down the road at Rotorua. Not too far away from your father.'

She'd spent too much time in Rotorua Hospital having treatment to ever want to work there. 'I considered it and flagged the idea.' So he hadn't just hitched a ride down to New Zealand on a whim. He'd done some research. Interesting. But how far should she go with what she told him? He was leaving in a few hours and she didn't know if he'd ever come back. Did he even need to know about her illness unless everything went pear-shaped?

'Are you a partner in the medical centre?' After looking along the road both ways, he edged the stroller over the kerb to cross the street.

'You're a natural at this kid stuff,' she teased, and laughed out loud at the stunned look on his face.

'You reckon? I've never taken a toddler for a walk in my life.' The stunned look became slightly smug and his chest puffed out a little.

'Hidden talents. Who'd have thought?' Then she pointed to a building further down the road. 'There's your rental company. And, no, I haven't taken a partnership but Dad's thinking about re-tiring soon and the other partners are keen for me to buy him out.'

She genuinely wanted to pay the going rate for Dad's share of the practice but so far hadn't been able to convince him of that idea. He kept telling her it was her inheritance and he didn't need the money anyway. 'We're also looking for another partner. Patient numbers are growing rapidly and it's hard to turn people away when they need our help.'

'I can understand that.' They'd reached the rental place. He stepped away from the stroller. 'I'll go and sort this car business out.'

She watched him saunter through the gleaming cars lined up facing the road. He walked with his back straight, his head high, shoulders back. Like a soldier. Her pathetic hint about another partner at the centre had been a waste of breath. Working there would be dull and monotonous for a man like Marshall.

Would he ever consider quitting the army and going into medicine full time? Doubtful. Even if he did return to civvie street it wouldn't be in New Zealand, and definitely not in a quiet town like Taupo. He was used to the excitement of war zones and the urgency of battlefield injuries, the variety of location and people. Taupo would never suit him.

Her stomach lurched. It had been pie-in-the-sky stuff to think they had a future together. She didn't even know if he liked her enough, let alone loved her. The fact he was her daughter's father wasn't grounds for marriage. Two weeks of hot sex and laughter in the sun weren't either.

How had she gone from talking about the medical centre to thinking about marriage? Because she loved him. Had always suspected that she'd fallen for him but with finding herself pregnant and then learning post-partum that she had cervical cancer her feelings for Marshall had been shoved into the too-hard basket.

She hadn't wanted to deal with the heartbreak of knowing she loved a man who almost didn't exist.

But less than twenty-four hours since he'd crashed back into her world she knew from the bottom of her heart that this was the man she loved, would always love. And the worst of it was that she didn't know what to do about it. Tell him and he'd most likely leave town without giving her any contact details at all. That must not happen. The day might come when Aimee would need him, when he might have to step up as the sole parent.

Toot, toot.

'You going my way, lady?' Marshall pulled up beside her in an SUV, grinning like a loon.

'Depends what you've got to offer.'

'You've got a short memory.' He winked at her.

Her stomach tightened. Heat crept up her cheeks as she recalled fingers and a tongue on her skin and a hard body covering hers.

'Or maybe not, if that smoky look in your eyes is anything to go by.' Chuckling, he climbed out and undid the straps keeping Aimee in her stroller. 'Come on, girls, hop in. I'm taking you to a café for coffee and juice.' His brows almost met in the middle of his forehead. 'How do we strap Aimee safely into the seat? She's far too tiny.'

'The stroller very cleverly becomes a car seat and we thread the SUV's seat belt through those clips.' Within moments she had it all sorted and Aimee safe. Turning to Marshall, she suggested, 'We could drive out to Huka Falls. You may as well see something of Taupo before you leave, and there's a café there.'

His finger tilted her head up and those sucker-in eyes locked with hers. 'I will be back, Charlie. I don't know when. It would be rash to make that sort of promise knowing the army as I do, but I will return.' He meant it. He really, really did. The truth, his honesty stared out at her.

It wasn't enough. Not nearly enough. She needed concrete dates for visits, not some vague idea that he'd return when it suited him or his superiors. But looking into his eyes, like peering into his soul, her breath stuck somewhere between her lungs and her lips, and she couldn't find the words to tell him what she needed.

Then her cellphone rang, shocking her back to the here and now of the rental company. Flipping the phone open, she saw it was Molly from the medical centre.

'Sorry, got to take this,' Charlie said to Marshall. 'Hey, what's up?' she asked the centre's receptionist.

'Emergency at the airport. A small plane with tandem skydivers on board crashed on take-off. The police are asking for any available doctors to proceed to the airport immediately. Can you go?'

'Yes. Hold on. I might have another doctor for you.' She looked at Marshall. 'There's been an accident and doctors are needed. Can you help? Under my guidance, of course, as you're not New Zealand registered.'

'What are we waiting for?' Marshall headed back round to the driver's door then changed his mind. 'Better for you to drive. That'll save time.'

Talking to Molly at the same time as slipping into the SUV, Charlie said, 'I'm on my way with another doctor. He'll have to work under supervision but I don't see a problem.'

'That's great. Where's your dad? I can't raise him.'

'He's out on the lake. I need to drop Aimee off with someone. I'm in town.'

'Got that covered. Gemma's here and says

she'll meet you at the airport. She'll bring you a medical bag and take Aimee home.'

Charlie slammed the gear lever into 'Drive' and snapped her seat belt on. 'Let's go.'

CHAPTER SIX

THE RIDE TO the airport would've been exciting if Marshall hadn't been considering the injuries they'd find when they got there.

Obviously Charlie was too because she hissed through clenched teeth, 'Impact injuries mean spinal damage, ruptured organs and broken bones.'

'For starters.' Marshall grimaced. 'You're presuming there are survivors.'

'We wouldn't have been called if there weren't.'

'True. I wonder what altitude the plane reached before something went wrong. It would've been moving at maximum speed and could've spun into the ground nose first.' Goose-bumps rose on his arms. He knew exactly what that looked like. 'We had a plane crash on landing at my last posting in Afghanistan so I've some idea of what to expect.'

'How did you cope? Did you know any of the men on that plane?'

'Yes.' He stared out the windscreen but it was the injured bodies of his men he saw. He could hear Rod groaning, could see his shaking hands splayed across his leaking wound. Marshall closed his eyes, drew air deep into his lungs and focused inwards. If only he'd been able to save his buddy then he wouldn't have this guilt of failure weighing him down. It could've happened to him, and still could one day. He couldn't put Charlie and Aimee through what Rod's family had had to deal with.

Charlie's soft voice slowly broke through his dark thoughts. 'I wonder how many people were on board. Usually there's a maximum of six sky-divers strapped together in pairs, and the pilot.'

Turning from staring outside to watching her, he asked, 'As the hospital here isn't a major one, what happens with the patients we attend?'

Indicating to turn left, Charlie slowed and turned into the airport grounds. 'Depending on the severity of the injuries, they'll be flown by helicopter to either Rotorua Hospital or Waikato Hospital up in Hamilton. Again, depending on the extent of injuries, one of us may have to accompany the patient or patients.'

A police car led them onto the grass perimeter. Ahead, black smoke spewed into the sky and fire trucks surrounded what had to be the wrecked plane. Ambulances were parked nearby, the back doors wide open as crews carried heavy packs of equipment towards the victims.

As Charlie pulled up beside the trucks she hauled in a deep breath and clenched her hands then loosened them. 'Here we go.' Shoving the door wide, she dropped to the ground and handed Aimee over to Gemma.

Jogging along beside her, Marshall took her free hand and squeezed it hard. 'You'll do fine. Once you get started, everything will slot into place. Just like you used to do in the ED.'

Then there was no more time to talk. They were at the site of the crash. Tangled metal that no longer resembled an aircraft stuck up out of the ground from the small crater the impact had made. Bodies lay everywhere.

'Hey, Charlie. Glad you're here,' Joseph, a doctor from another medical centre in town, called to her. He crossed to them and shook Marshall's hand when she introduced the two men. She recognised the other doctor and a nurse already working with victims. 'I've been put in charge of the scene. We've triaged the poor devils who are lucky to be alive. Two dead. Four in a very bad way. We need to crack on.'

'Where do you want us? You understand that

Marshall is an American army doctor without registration here?' She'd had Molly relay the information earlier.

Joseph nodded at Marshall. 'You're probably more qualified for this scenario than the rest of us. You two take that couple by the firemen. They're still strapped together in preparation for their dive.'

The male and female victims had been slammed into the ground, their bodies tangled together and bound by the parachute straps. Both were unconscious. 'Barely alive,' Charlie muttered, after finding very weak carotid pulses in both.

'Freeing them won't be easy,' Marshall muttered. 'We could cause more damage but there's no helping that. Let's start the ABCs.'

They dropped to their knees and began checking airways, breathing rates, pulses. Charlie automatically went for the young woman. At least she presumed the girl was young. Hard to tell with the facial injuries.

She looked around for one of the ambulance crew. 'Can we have two neck braces?' They'd need to put the braces on before trying to separate their patients and move them. She began a thorough examination of the woman, not easy when there was a man strapped to her back.

'Soft bone on the side of her skull, broken cheekbones.' Her hands moved down the neck, over her patient's arms. 'Broken right humerus, crushed ribs, palpable spleen.'

Marshall reported similar injuries in the places he could reach on his patient. With the help of two ambulance officers they placed the neck braces on, before supervising the firemen as they cut the straps and removed the parachute from the man's back.

'Slowly does it,' Marshall cautioned as the woman was placed carefully on a stretcher. Immediately Charlie began another check of the woman's vital signs. 'Blood pressure's dropping, resp rate's falling.' Suddenly there were no heartbeats. 'Cardiac arrest,' she yelled, and began CPR. Nodding at one of the ambulance officers, she gasped, 'Need an airway in place, attach a mask and bag. Someone get the defib.' Fifteen, sixteen, seventeen. She continued counting the compressions as the ambulance officer slipped the plastic airway into the patient's mouth and then strapped a mask over her face.

'Twenty-nine, thirty.' Charlie sat back, watched as the oxygen bag was squeezed twice. Leaning forward, she folded one hand over the other and began the next round of compressions while a paramedic placed the defib pads on the woman's now exposed chest.

'Stand back,' he ordered quietly but firmly.

Charlie stopped the compressions and moved away from her patient. She continued compressions when the electric shock did not restart the heart. Another shock, more compressions.

'I'm not giving up,' she muttered, more to herself than anyone else.

'I've got a pulse.' The paramedic sounded relieved.

She could relate to that. 'Right, let's finish the assessment and do what's necessary before sending this lady off to hospital. Where's Joseph?'

'Right here. Want to fly her to Waikato?'

'A.S.A.P.' Oh, hell. The monitors attached to the woman reading her heart rate gave a warning. 'Here we go again.' The blood loss from those internal injuries had to be huge, causing the heart to stop.

They got the woman's heart going again, gained large-bore IV access to give fluids for shock and made her ready for evacuation. The paramedics whisked her over to a waiting helicopter for her flight to Waikato Hospital's major trauma unit.

Charlie joined Marshall as he was splinting

both his patient's legs. She held the cardboard splint while he strapped it tight enough to be effective without cutting off any blood supply.

'How're you doing?' she asked quietly.

'Like I'm not on holiday.' He flicked a grim smile. 'I thought you said Taupo was a quiet place.'

'Yeah, well, usually.' She looked across at the wreckage and shuddered. The impact had concertinaed the plane to a fraction of its original length. 'I've got to go with my patient.' Glancing across, she saw the ambulance crew loading the stretcher into the helicopter.

His mouth tightened. 'How will you get back from wherever you're going?'

'The pilot will wait while I hand over. I'll be away two hours max.' She glanced at her watch and her skin turned to ice. Two hours and Marshall would be gone. They still had so much to talk about. She hadn't even got his contact details. Her teeth dug into her bottom lip as she stood up on surprisingly shaky legs.

'Charlie.' Joseph tapped her on the shoulder. 'Your flight's about to lift off.'

'I refuse to say goodbye, Marshall. Please call me as soon as you get back to the States.' Kissing her fingers, she touched Marshal's cheek and turned and ran fast. Towards the patient who needed all her skills, away from the man who owned her heart. Would she ever see him again?

Marshall drove carefully on State Highway One towards Auckland and his flight back to the States. He had covered nearly half the distance, and with every kilometre his heart grew heavier. He was leaving something very special behind. A wonderful family who'd welcomed him with open arms.

Hell, working together on those casualties had been like old times. Charlie's skills had improved no end despite not working in emergency medicine. Her confidence had grown a lot over the years.

Mindful of which side of the road he was on, he tried not to think about Charlie and their abrupt parting. Despite being used to the suddenness of changing circumstances in combat zones, he had not been prepared for the sudden departure of Charlie from his life only hours ago.

It was little more than twenty-four hours since he'd seen her for the first time in a long time. It had been like finding someone he hadn't known he'd lost until that moment—his other half. They'd fitted together instantly. There'd been no real awkwardness after the first few minutes. Not even the shock of learning about Aimee had driven a wedge between them or made him want to get away—except for a few brief, confused minutes.

Yet now he was on his way, leaving this country and his daughter and Charlie. Charlotte Lang. Her image had tormented him for years, colouring his dreams, unsettling his long-held beliefs. He'd truly thought he could come over here, spend a little time with her and walk away completely over what ailed him.

The oath that shot out of his mouth shocked even him, seasoned soldier that he was. He'd been a fool. Rod had warned him time and again that he was hooked but he'd disputed that, saying it wasn't possible to fall in love in two weeks. How could he love a woman he didn't know anything about apart from her stunning body and its fantastic reactions to his lovemaking?

But none of that mattered. He had to go. That's what he did, had always done. Moved on. It had never been a problem before. He'd never cared before. He had men depending on him back home so between here and Auckland he needed to pull on his army persona and start acting like the competent officer he was. He could definitely not behave like some lovelorn fool who was leaving behind the most wonderful woman he'd ever met and the sweet little girl he'd fathered. The only way to get through life without hurting others was to remain alone.

Hamilton. The road sign indicated he should carry on straight ahead.

Auckland. Turn right to bypass the city.

Marshall indicated a right-hand turn. He didn't need the delays that driving through a city would bring.

You didn't find out why deep sadness unexpectedly sneaked into Charlie's eyes at times.

Yeah, buddy, I hear you. Unfortunately it didn't work out. That plane crash took care of the last few hours I had with her.

Don't you want to know? Or is running away preferable to what Charlie might tell you?

Stop mucking with my head. I've got to concentrate on driving. These Kiwis aren't very forgiving motorists.

Excuses, excuses.

He wasn't running away. He didn't do that. The SUV slowed. He glanced at the dials on the dashboard. All normal. What was happening? He pressed down on the accelerator and the vehicle surged forward and maintained a steady one hundred kilometres an hour. Idiot.

Why had he lifted his foot off the pedal? Slowing his departure?

The soft sensation he'd felt when Charlie had brushed her kissed fingertips over his cheek drifted through his mind. Charlie. They'd shared two kisses in these past hours. Kisses filled with hunger, longing, caring. Kisses that had held so much promise.

Pulling to the side of the road, he switched the engine off. He couldn't drive and deal with all this stuff going on in his head at the same time. So if he wasn't running, why leave? No one had ordered him to head back to Kansas today. The army had called and he'd jumped. A habit formed from following orders for too long. Orders designed to save a man's life in combat. Orders that took serious decision-making away if a man let it.

As you have.

'Damn it, Rod, can't you go and annoy someone else?' He slapped the steering-wheel. If he turned round and went back to Charlie, would she read too much into it? Expect more of him than he was prepared to give? His gut churned as fear of getting too involved reared up.

Reaching for the ignition, he hesitated. Withdrew his hand. Asked himself a scary question.

'What do I want to do? If I was free of the army, would I go back to Charlie without a thought?'

Hard to imagine being free of the army when it had been more of a family to him than his folks had. But it was an impersonal, unloving institution. This wasn't about getting out, only about returning to Charlie for a few more days.

Family. The word evoked things he'd missed out on and the hidden dreams that one day his parents might've remembered to acknowledge they'd had a son they loved. He'd spent his childhood trying to be noticed for the right reasons, but some things just didn't work out in life, no matter how hard a guy tried.

You could try to change. Make the most of this opportunity.

Opportunity. That was one word for what waited for him in Taupo. Commitment was another. Could he commit to being in Charlie and Aimee's lives from a distance? Stay safe for them? He wasn't going to know unless he tried. His hand wasn't as steady as it normally was when he reached for the ignition this time. A vision of Charlie filtered into his mind. She'd been awesome, the way she hadn't demanded anything of him for Aimee.

But it was her steady blue gaze that really got to him. Full of understanding, need and sadness. Occasionally tinged with laughter and something that shot straight to his heart and grabbed it. Love? Did Charlie love him? Not likely. But maybe she cared a lot about him. That was something he wasn't used to.

The engine turned over and he flicked on the indicator. When a break came in the traffic Marshall made a U-turn.

He wasn't finished with Charlie Lang. Not by a long shot.

Dad stuffed the trout with lemon zest and garlic then wrapped it in foil. 'That'll go on the barbecue shortly. Want a salad with it?'

Charlie nodded. 'Sure.' Like she cared. She doubted she'd taste a thing. Marshall had gone. At least he'd left an email address so she could contact him. Considering how much effort she'd put into trying to find an address, she should be grateful. She wasn't. Not at all. They hadn't talked through anything to do with Aimee. They hadn't talked at all.

'Charlotte.' Dad sat down at the kitchen table beside her.

When he called her Charlotte she knew she should listen, but today she didn't want to. What could Dad say that would make her feel any better? Raising one eyebrow, she grimaced.

'He promised me he wouldn't hurt you or Aimee.'

'Goes to show how much his promises mean, doesn't it?' She shoved her chair back and went to get a glass of water.

'I believed him. Still do. It wasn't Marshall's fault his flight was brought forward or that you had to fly to Waikato Hospital with your patient. Give him a break, love.'

Leaning back against the bench, she studied the inside of her glass. 'I can do that. But can I expect to see him again? I haven't told him everything. He needs to know why it's important he stays in touch.' She shouldn't have avoided the issue when she'd had the chance during their walk into town. But it had seemed too soon, a huge information dump when he had still been coming to terms with Aimee's existence.

'I don't believe you've seen or heard the last of him.'

'I only hope you're right.' She poured the water down her throat, hoping her father didn't see the threatening tears at the corners of her eyes. She'd stupidly admitted to herself that she loved Marshall and now she had to somehow forget that and get on with her life. The first time she'd done it, it had been hard enough. This time felt infinitely worse. They shared a child now. 'I'll take Aimee out to her paddling pool.' And try to gain some semblance of control over these feelings of despair.

Aimee loved water. So much so it worried Charlie at times. Smacking the water so that it splashed everywhere made Aimee burst into shrieks of laughter. Despite her mood, Charlie couldn't help smiling at her girl. 'Go for it, sweetheart.' She eased herself onto a garden chair by the small plastic pool.

'She's a water baby, just like her mom,' drawled a familiar American accent.

She shot off the chair so fast she tripped and would've fallen on her butt if Marshall hadn't caught her.

He laughed and said, 'You're obviously glad to see me.' And then he kissed her. Thoroughly. So that her muscles and bones liquefied. So that she forgot everything except the man whose arms were holding her upright, whose hard, lean body supported her. A bubble of desire and need and love rolled up her throat and burst across her lips to be caught in his mouth.

He pulled his mouth away enough to utter, 'God, Charlie, I've missed you,' and then went back to kissing her.

He'd missed her? Yes. A mental fist went up in the air. For more than two years? Or a few hours? Whatever. He was back. For how long? Did it matter when he'd made the effort to return? She slid her hands behind his neck and held on for all she was worth.

'Guess I should be getting the beers,' Dad growled from somewhere behind them.

Marshall slowly lifted his head, withdrawing that delicious mouth as though reluctant to stop kissing her. 'Yes, sir, that would be great.' And then he kissed her again, a quick kiss on her lips before putting her down on her feet. 'I like your dad.'

Dad probably felt a teeny bit smug right now, with Marshall's sudden reappearance. She asked, 'How far did you get?'

'The turn-off for Auckland outside Hamilton.'

'What happened? Did your flight get changed again?'

He took her hand and tugged her across to the lounger on the veranda where he sat and lifted her onto his lap, holding her there with an arm around her waist. He needn't have worried. She wasn't going anywhere.

'I bailed. Told the guys I'll find my own way back to the States later. If it's all right with you, I'd like to hang around and get to know my daughter.' Then he added, 'Actually, I'd like to get to know her mom even better.'

Warmth flooded her. Yes, this was what she'd hoped for. 'You can stay here.' He would, wouldn't he? It made sense.

His eyes narrowed. 'Are you sure that's a good idea? Hadn't you better check with Brendon first?'

'Check what with me?' Dad asked as he strolled out, two beers in one hand.

'Marshall's staying for two weeks and I said he could bunk down here.'

'I should think so.' Then he added, 'But don't let us pressure you, lad. You might find you want time to yourself.'

'Then I'll go for a run, or have a beer at the hotel. Thank you both. That's settled.'

Marshall had returned. That's all Charlie knew. And she was happy to accept that, to enjoy his company. At least she had time up her sleeve now. She could afford to give him some space. As long as they didn't share too many of those hot kisses. Otherwise all her good intentions would combust.

Now, there was a thought. Her smile felt smug even to her.

CHAPTER SEVEN

MONDAY MORNING AND the bedside alarm screeched into Charlie's sleep-soaked brain. Six o'clock. She jerked upright. Something wasn't right. Again Aimee hadn't woken her. She used the alarm clock as back-up.

Leaping out of bed, she threw her robe around her shoulders as she raced down the hall to Aimee's bedroom. What had happened? Was she okay? Her heart thudded hard against her ribs as she ran into the bedroom. She pulled up in a hurry. Aimee's cot was empty.

That had to be good. Didn't it? Had Marshall got Aimee up again? Back out in the hall Charlie strode fast to the kitchen. And slammed to a stop in the doorway.

Dressed in running shorts and a tight tee shirt, Marshall sat at the table with a mug of what looked like black coffee in one hand. Aimee bounced on his knee, held firmly in place with his other hand. The smile beaming out at Aimee from her father stopped Charlie's heart. Filled with awe and happiness and care—or was that love?—his mouth curved into the sweetest smile she'd ever seen and his eyes glowed with emotion. He really had no problem accepting Aimee was his child. He'd embraced the concept, not once questioning if she was sure.

She opened her mouth to say something but the words stuck in her throat. Never in all the months of searching for this man had she believed he'd fall for his daughter so easily, so quickly.

'Look who's woken up.' Marshall spoke to Aimee but his eyes had focused on Charlie. 'Aimee was a wee bit grizzly so I figured it would be okay to get her up. But by the look on your face, I guess I did wrong.'

'Not at all.' She drew breath to get her emotions under control. No point giving him any clues as to how she felt about him yet. If ever. Now he was getting the hang of being a parent he might start thinking of wanting more kids, which would lead to even more problems. Her heart squeezed. She'd love more of Marshall's babies. Gulp. Concentrate on what they were talking about, not the impossible.

On an indrawn breath she said, 'Aimee usually wakes me up, so when the alarm went off

I thought something had happened to her.' Her mild panic sounded stupid, even over the top, now. Trying for a nonchalant shrug, she crossed to the hot kettle and flicked the switch to make tea. Then she plopped a kiss on Aimee's grinning face. 'Morning, sweetheart.'

'Do I get one?'

'Sure.' She leaned closer, kissed Marshall's stubbly chin. 'Morning.'

The hand that had been holding his mug now gripped her arm and held her in place while his mouth reached for hers. 'We can do better than that.' And then he was kissing her. Again. This was getting to be a habit. A habit she enjoyed.

Aimee grabbed a handful of Charlie's hair and pulled hard. 'Mum, mum.'

'Ouch.' She stepped back a pace. 'Careful, little one. Mummy's head hurts when you do that.' Her scalp had been tender since the day her hair had fallen out due to the chemo. Blinking rapidly, she turned away from Marshall's all-seeing gaze and concentrated on making tea.

When she sat at the table with her drink, she'd got her emotions in order again. 'You're an early riser,' she commented to Marshall.

'Like to go for a run before it gets too hot.' He jiggled Aimee on his knees and was rewarded with giggles. 'But I got sidetracked this morning.'

'I can understand that. She's always been a great time-waster. But if you want to go out you can put her down. We'll be showering as soon as I've had my tea. Aimee usually joins me.' It was the fastest and easiest way to get her girl washed.

Marshall's face lit up. 'A family affair.'

Her cheeks heated up. 'You needn't think you're joining us.'

He scowled exaggeratedly and held a hand over his heart. 'Ow, she wounds so easily.'

'Go on with you. I'm still getting used to you being here. I'm certainly not ready for anything more intimate yet.'

'Yet? So there's a possibility? If I behave?' His grin turned wicked. As did the glint in his eyes.

'You don't know how to behave.'

'Is that so? Talk about a challenge.' His grin only widened. Any further and he was in danger of splitting the corners of that delectable mouth she so enjoyed kissing.

'Go for your run. I haven't got time to sit around talking nonsense at this hour of the day. I've got to get ready for work.'

He wiggled his eyebrows at her. 'Nonsense? Did you hear that, Aimee? Your mom's a hard woman. Take it from me.' Then his face settled back to near normal. 'Have you got time to join me on the run?'

Yes, she did but was she up to it? 'I'll be too slow.'

'Let's give it a shot. We can turn back any time you've had enough.' Definitely a challenge twinkling out at her.

In the past she'd have taken him up on it, but now, after everything she'd been through? 'I'll be turning back. You can keep pounding the pavement for your usual time. I'll tell Dad.'

'What time do you leave for work?'

'A little after eight. Aimee goes with me. We've got a crèche at the centre for staff families, as well as for patients' children so they can have a more relaxed consultation.'

'Exactly how little after eight?'

She shrugged. 'Five, ten minutes, maybe more. I go when I'm ready.'

Annoyance battled with bewilderment in his face. 'What time do you start work, then?'

'When I get there.' She chuckled as it dawned on her what Marshall's problem was. 'At the medical centre we aren't regimented. It's not a standing order to arrive exactly at eight-thirty. As long as we're there on time for our first appointments at nine no one has any concerns. I like to spend half an hour or so looking up test results that have come in overnight, check who I'm seeing and going over their medical histories. But if I don't have time before the day gets under way it's not the end of the world. I do those things as I go.' Draining her mug, she stood and reached for Aimee. 'Come on, little one. Let's find Granddad.'

'But working to a strict timetable saves a lot of wasted time and many mistakes.' Marshall also stood and gathered up their mugs, placing them in the sink.

'Sounds too stifling for me.'

'It works for the armed forces. There'd be no end of problems if we weren't so controlled. Imagine telling the men to draw arms and have them doing it as it suited them.' He shook his head. 'Impossible.'

She smiled at his serious countenance. 'Although there are times when it feels like it, the medical centre is not a war zone.'

'I guess.' Then he relaxed and his heart-wrenching smile returned. 'You might even have a point. Yesterday at the airport it was amazing how everyone worked together without anyone issuing constant directions. People knew what had to be done and got on with it, helping each other, giving the patients the utmost in care.'

The smile turned wry. 'I had to bite my tongue a couple of times when I was about to yell an order only to find whatever I thought needed doing was already being done. It wasn't my place to say anything, but it wouldn't have stopped me.'

No surprise there. 'There's more than one way of getting the best out of people.' She headed for the door. 'Sorry, but I haven't got time to sit around talking all morning. I'm going for a run.'

'Are you sure you're up to this?' Worry glinted out of Dad's eyes. 'Running's hard on the body when you're not used to it.'

'I'll only do about four or five k's. If that.'

'I don't know.'

'I'll be fine. Promise.' Dad had become over-protective. Who could blame him? He'd lost his beloved wife to cancer and lived in terror of losing her. But she couldn't go on not trying to get back to being the fit person she'd once been.

The sun mightn't be up to speed in its intensity but the morning was still hot. The sweat poured off Marshall as he pounded the footpath down to the lake. Glancing sideways, he got a shock to find Charlie hadn't kept up with him. Slowing to jog on the spot, he waited for her to catch up. 'You were serious about being out of practice.'

Her chest rose and fell rapidly. 'Yes,' she gasped. 'I'll turn back now.' Her disappointment was obvious.

Stopping his jogging completely, Marshall took her hand and began walking along the path. 'Deep breaths.' When her fingers curled around his hand, warmth stole through him and settled around his heart. 'You did fine for your first time out in a while.' He doubted they'd come as far as she'd hoped but he wouldn't put a dampener on her attempt. 'Want to walk or run home?'

'Definitely walk. I can't believe how hard that was. To think I used to run for an hour and not feel too bad. You have no idea how angry that makes me feel.'

'So why didn't you get back into running once Aimee was born?'

'Long story.' Tugging her hand free, she added, 'Talk to you later. I'll be late if I don't get a move on.'

'I'll come with you.'

Her hand came up in a stop signal. 'No way. Carry on. I'll see you soon.' And she turned for home.

He wanted to go with her and demand an explanation because he got the impression there was a lot she hadn't told him yet. A long story she'd said, with sadness creeping into her voice and eyes. Pushing her might get the answers he craved but could also make her tetchy with him. So he'd continue his run and try to talk to her later.

Anyway, he needed the exercise. Nothing like a hard run to loosen his muscles and get him ready for the day. Not that he knew how he'd fill in the hours until Charlie came home from the medical centre.

Unless he offered to take care of Aimee for a while. Get to know his little girl. She fascinated him, so cute and small. He could take photos. Mom and Dad might like to see them. Yeah, right. If they hadn't had time for him it was very unlikely they'd be bothered about Aimee. Especially as she lived halfway round the world from their usual haunts.

They'd be the losers. Not him. Even if he didn't become a regular feature in his child's life he'd make sure she knew he loved her. Like how? Emails, computer video calls, phone calls when she was older, birthday and Christmas presents. It didn't sound like enough. Would he have been satisfied with that when he'd been growing up? Hell, he'd got the presents and phone calls and, no, he hadn't been at all happy.

Marshall shivered. Balancing this parenting lark with his army life wasn't going to be easy. It didn't help that he lived in a different country from Charlie and Aimee. Would Charlie consider moving to the States? Not fair to ask her. She'd be lonely and miss her support network of Brendon and friends. Besides, she had her career here, was set up for life really.

He increased his pace, trying to outrun his thoughts, and for a while he succeeded. Finally he turned for home. Damn. Turned for Charlie's home. They were sucking him in with their kindness, openness and honesty. No pressure about what he wanted to do now he knew he was a dad. Nothing like that at all. Just make himself at home and go with the flow. So alien for him. Yet he kind of liked it. Could even get used to it.

At the gate into the large section where Charlie's home stood he flicked the childproof lock and walked through as though he'd always done this. As if coming home to a wonderful woman and his child was normal.

Hell, turn around and run away, fast. But no. His feet kept moving in the direction of the front door. He'd shower and have breakfast before taking over looking after Aimee for a while. How hard could that be?

* * *

Charlie laughed fit to bust. 'I think you'll have to try a more hands-on approach.'

Marshall looked from Aimee to her and back again, confusion gleaming in his eyes. 'Hands on?'

Slipping the strap of her laptop case over her shoulder, she reached for the car keys hanging on the hook just inside the kitchen door. Still laughing, she told him, 'You can't insist that Aimee goes pee pee. Learning to use the potty is still a bit of a mystery to her.'

'Truly?' He looked stunned.

She couldn't help adding, 'She's not an army recruit. You have to take her to the bathroom, remove her pants and sit her down on the pot.'

'You don't think I can do this, do you?' The smile returned but didn't quite reach his eyes. He was seeing this as a challenge. Not good for either him or Aimee.

Stepping over to him, she placed a hand on his arm, squeezed gently. 'I would never leave my daughter with someone I didn't believe capable of caring for her. Not even her father.'

He glowered at her. 'You're trying to con me, babe.'

'Yep. Totally.' Up on tiptoe she planted a kiss on his now clean-shaven chin. 'See you both later at the centre.' As she strode away she added quietly, 'All clean and tidy with big smiles on your faces.'

'I heard that.' Marshall stood at the kitchen door, Aimee on his hip. 'You are so in for a surprise, Charlotte Lang.'

She hoped so. Waving her hand over her shoulder in his direction, she headed outside. Another glorious day and Marshall was here. Still here. He'd shocked her when he'd returned last night. Not to mention warming her from the bottom of her stomach right through to her heart. He certainly didn't shy away from responsibilities, even those he'd had dumped on him only the day before.

It felt weird going into work without Aimee accompanying her. But within minutes of parking at the back of the building she'd explained to the girl running the crèche that Aimee would be in later and quickly became absorbed in laboratory results and radiology findings. Aimee and Marshall were firmly at the back of her mind by the time she read an abnormal mammogram result for a patient of hers. Keisha Harris was in her mid-thirties and had two gorgeous boys she adored. She'd gone to school with Charlie, been in the same netball team, gone out clubbing with the same friends.

And now she might have the same bloody disease. If further tests came back positive then, despite a different part of Keisha's body being affected, it would still disrupt Keisha's life as badly as it had hers.

With a heavy heart Charlie picked up the phone and dialled Keisha's home number. When the answering-machine picked up she went to ask Molly, 'Do you know if Keisha's working during the school holidays? I need to speak to her.' As soon as possible.

'She and Toby have taken the boys to Phuket for two weeks. I think they're due home at the end of the week.'

'I'll leave a message on her phone that hopefully won't cause alarm.' What were the chances of that? She had to make Keisha aware she needed to get in touch fairly quickly. The radiology centre had probably left a message recalling Keisha for further X-rays. There wasn't any point in disrupting the family's holiday, though. One week wouldn't make any difference and they might as well make the most of their fun time because the next few weeks were going to be tough while Keisha underwent tests and waited for results.

Molly told her, 'Your first patient's here.'

Charlie dealt with prescription renewals, a

sprained ankle and a mildly depressed teen before Mrs Withers slipped into her room, complaining of chest pains. With Gemma's help Charlie ran tests and promptly called an ambulance to take their patient to hospital.

Next six-year-old Josh Donaldson bounced in, every bit of exposed skin covered with what looked like hives. Scratching like mad at his arms, he grizzled, 'I don't like these bumps. They sting and make me stay awake at night.'

'I don't blame you for not liking them.' Charlie studied his red, puffy skin. 'What did he have to eat before these started appearing?' she asked his mother, Vicki.

His mum looked distressed at the thought she'd fed her son something he might be allergic to. 'Nothing out of the ordinary. Chicken sandwiches, ice cream and peaches. He's never shown a reaction to any food before.'

Charlie smiled across at Vicki. 'Being a mother doesn't get any easier, does it? Every time I think I'm making headway with Aimee she tosses up something different for me to deal with.' So far health issues hadn't been a problem, but she crossed her fingers anyway. 'She's started climbing everything in sight.' Which wasn't good when there was a road outside the front gate.

'I know exactly what you mean. It's like a minefield. I thought that once Josh was old enough to go to school he wouldn't be having any problems. Shows how much I know.' Vicki ran her hand lovingly over her son's head.

Charlie turned to the boy. 'Josh, where were you playing yesterday?'

'Dad took us to the river for a swim.' Scratch, scratch. 'I saw an eel and my sister cried when she slipped on the rocks.' He grinned, with no sympathy for little Karla whatsoever.

'No sand flies? Bees? Wasps?' When the boy shook his head she continued, 'I'll arrange for an allergy test to be done by one of our nurses. It will take about an hour. And I'll give you some cream to take the itch and heat out of those bumps.'

Josh asked, 'Can Gemma do it? I like her best.'

'I'm sure she can.'

Vicki and Josh disappeared back to Reception to make an appointment with Gemma.

Charlie went in search of her next patient and bumped into her father in the hall. 'Why are you here so early?'

His eyes lit up. 'I've been replaced at home. My breakfast was waiting when I came out of my room. Aimee was in her highchair, firing pieces of toast around the kitchen and quite happy to be waited on by Marshall, who looked as though being out on a recce with his troop would be a whole lot easier than dealing with an eighteen-month-old.'

She chuckled. 'Wish I'd been a fly on the wall.'

'Can't you at least pretend to feel sorry for him?'

Pressing her lips together, she shook her head. 'Nope. It's good for him.'

'You're a hard woman, Charlotte Lang.'

'Wonder where I learned that?' She walked into the waiting room and looked around the patients. 'Kathy, come on through.'

By eleven Charlie was more than ready for a coffee and biscuit. As her previous patient disappeared Gemma stepped through the door, her eyes wide and bulging.

'I thought the Greeks had it sussed when it came to male gods. But I'm telling you, there's a hunk out in Reception, holding Aimee, who puts all those statues to shame.'

And that's with his clothes on. Charlie's stomach tightened as she smiled. 'Am I right in thinking he might be about six-three, broad shoulders tapering down to slim hips, buzz-cut hairstyle and a face to get lost in?'

'That's the one. Aimee's plastered all over him as though she's never going to let him go.'

Charlie's smile slipped. That could be a problem. 'I'd better go and rescue her. Or should that be him?'

Gemma laughed. 'Charlie, you've been hiding out on me. I know you said Aimee's dad was one of a kind, but I never got an inkling just how wow he really is.'

'Dribbling doesn't suit you.' Running a hand over her hair, she slipped around her desk, excitement fizzing along her veins. It hadn't been three hours since she'd last seen Marshall but it was impossible to deny the need crawling through her. To see him, kiss him, touch him. Oops. Hold on. She was at work.

'Hey, did Marshall come right out and say he was Aimee's father? To everyone?'

Gemma stood blocking the doorway, a wide smile on her face. 'Yes, he did. Looked quite pleased with himself, too. He's gone through to the kitchen with Brendon to meet everyone. Your man seems to be getting on well with your dad.'

Her man? If only. 'They do get on, but I think Dad's working on buttering him up for a long-term plan that will work for both Aimee and me.'

'Sounds like Brendon, always thinking ahead.'

'That reminds me. Dad thinks you're pretty good, too. I just wanted to say if you're interested in getting close to him, go for it. I heartily approve.' Good-natured, sweet-hearted, happy-go-lucky Gemma would be perfect for Dad.

Gemma. Someone she owed so much to. She'd spent hours sitting with her as she'd puked her stomach dry after rounds of chemo. It was Gemma who'd gone shopping for wigs with her, and had laughed until she'd cried when a wig had got whipped off her head as she'd ducked under a low-hanging branch one day. Gemma had held her hand and listened to all her fears for Aimee and Dad. Gemma, fifteen years older than her and yet the best friend she'd ever had.

Gemma's hug enveloped her. 'Didn't think you'd mind. Now, go and claim that hunk out in the kitchen before one of the other females in this building hustles him away.'

CHAPTER EIGHT

EARLY TUESDAY MORNING Charlie got dressed in her running gear. 'I can't believe how much my muscles ache,' she grumbled as she jogged beside Marshall. 'It's going to take weeks to get fit.'

'Toughen up.' He nudged her gently and when she flipped her head up he was grinning at her.

'Easy for you to say.' She glanced at his long legs, which were eating up the metres no problem at all. One stride of his equalled almost two of hers. 'I've got an idea. Tomorrow I'll ride my bike while you run. Then we'll see who's fastest.'

His laughter made her happy and caused him to lose his breathing pattern. She laughed in return when he had to stop to sort his lungs out and she got a little way ahead. Not for long, though.

'Going my way?' He waved as he raced past. Her lungs were hurting and her legs protesting. Wishing she could take up the challenge, she wheezed out, 'I'm heading home. See you later.'

He turned and ran backwards for a moment. 'I'll bring lunch in to work.'

'We'll go down to the lake.'

A little after midday Charlie swallowed a mouthful of panini filled with salad and chicken and asked Marshall, 'What did you find to talk about to the other doctors all afternoon yesterday?'

'Medical stuff. You'd be surprised what other doctors want to know about the trauma cases I deal with out in the field.' Marshall chewed a blade of grass and gazed out over the sparkling wavelets the light breeze was churning up on the lake. 'I don't give a lot of detail but I guess it seems exciting compared to the routine of a clinic. What they don't get is that there are days I'd happily swap places. At least most of your patients won't have lost a limb or have holes blasted in their torsos by random gunfire.'

Charlie put her food aside, suddenly not hungry. 'How do you deal with that all the time?' Marshall rarely talked about his medical duties.

'I try to think about the guys I'm helping and put the rest aside.'

'Like that works.' Disappointment at being fobbed off grabbed at her. He'd finally said something personal and then backed away the moment she'd picked up on it.

He turned a grim face to her. 'Not a bit.'

She gasped at the raw pain in his eyes. 'Marshall?' she whispered, as she wrapped her hand around his much larger one. Small tremors shook him. His skin felt clammy and cold. His chest rose and fell on short breaths.

'It doesn't matter,' he croaked.

'Yeah, it does.' She looked around at Aimee, playing happily with the stones at the edge of the bank. 'Tell me,' she said.

His hand turned to cover hers, his grip intense. 'You remember Rod? My best buddy?' When she nodded he continued in a low voice, 'Two months after we left Hawaii we were in Afghanistan.' His Adam's apple bobbed. 'A plane carrying half my troop crashed at the end of the runway. Rod didn't make it. I tried everything I could to save him. Finally put him on the casualty flight out to Germany. I never saw him again.'

What could she say? Nothing that would help. She knew how hard people tried to make you feel better with words when your world had imploded. Words that usually just didn't work, didn't soothe or cure. She tightened her hold on his hand and leaned her head against his shoulder. 'I'm sorry.'

'Me, too.' His tongue slicked across his bottom lip. 'The worst of it? He knew he'd be dead before he got home so he wanted to stay on base with me. But I insisted he went, hoping beyond belief that he'd somehow make it to see his wife and boys. Who knows? Maybe I could've saved him. Or at least held his hand and talked with him.' His voice trailed off. His eyes were focused somewhere thousands of kilometres away, seeing something she'd never see.

'You're blaming yourself for something you couldn't prevent.'

'I mightn't have been flying that damned plane but I should've been able to hold him together long enough to get to a major hospital.'

'In another country.'

'It's why I became a doctor. To save people.' His voice sounded clogged with tears.

'You're the man who once told me we can't save them all.' Charlie rubbed her fingers back and forth across his hand.

'I should've been able to save my closest friend.'

'We can't save them all,' she repeated quietly yet firmly. He mustn't go on blaming himself.

This could destroy him if he let it. Lifting her head, she kissed his neck, his cheek, his lips.

Marshall gripped Charlie's hand, held on. Her lips were soft, sweet, caring. Touching him deep inside somewhere around his heart. Warming the cold place locked in there, no matter how many months had gone by since Rod had been loaded onto that flight.

Her touch was totally in contrast to the harsh reality of his life, of what he'd told her. Why the hell had he spilled his guts? It was the last thing he should be saying. He didn't do heart-to-heart stuff. Never had, never would. Except that's exactly what he'd just done.

A stone banged against his knee and rolled down his leg to his foot. Aimee stood on his other side, holding out her empty hand, grinning that cute grin that got to him every time. 'Hey, my girl, come here.' Wrapping his free arm around her, he tucked his daughter in against his side. Aimee on one side, Charlie on the other. The perfect picture, a family portrait. Alien. And the reason he had to keep surviving in the next place the army posted him to. And the next. And the next.

He'd be gone by the end of next week and he didn't have a clue when he'd be able to get to Taupo again. Charlie would be hurt. But not half as much as she would be if she thought they had a future together and then he got himself killed. He'd do what he could for Aimee, mostly the small stuff. But a full-on, day-by-day commitment? Not likely. These two were better off without him.

Charlie didn't sleep much that night. Tossing and turning, throwing the bedcovers off because she was too hot, pulling them back when the sweat on her skin chilled. Every time she closed her eyes she saw the anguish on Marshall's face, heard the pain in his voice as he'd talked about Rod.

Used to him always laughing and joking, she'd been shocked that he'd opened up at all. But she'd also been grateful because it meant they might be able to forge a deeper friendship, something strong enough to carry them through the months and years ahead.

Forget that she loved him. Yeah, right. Like how? Okay, her love wasn't going to vaporise or leave her in peace, but she had to take her time with that. First things first. Give Marshall the space to fall in love with his daughter. Because no matter that her own heart was his, Aimee had to take precedence.

The morning finally dawned, rays of sun

sneaking around the edges of her blinds just after five. Long before Aimee cried out or the alarm beeped, she crawled out of bed. A cool shower might wake her up and refresh her head, which felt full of cotton wool. Sodden, heavy cotton wool.

'Hey, you look like something the dog buried.' Marshall stood outside his bedroom door, watching as she shuffled along the hall yawning so hard her jaw ached. 'Didn't sleep?'

Shaking her head, she pushed the bathroom door wide. 'Too hot.'

Those all-seeing eyes bored into her, filled with concern. 'You're not worrying about anything, are you, Charlie?'

Only how I'm going to get through the day on very little shut-eye, how Aimee will react when you leave us, how I'll cope if you don't stay in touch. 'Thinking about one of my patients.'

She lied because now wasn't the time to tell him the truth. He would hate it if she put pressure on him, asked him exactly what he thought he might do about seeing Aimee occasionally. Or more often. Then there was the biggie. Would he sign papers accepting responsibility for Aimee in the worst-case scenario? Hopefully the untruth wasn't glittering out at him from her tired eyes. She'd have looked away but it was as though his gaze had locked onto hers, keeping her in place.

Annoyance flickered over his face. 'Really?'

Had he guessed she'd fibbed? Or did he want her to have been worried about the situation after all? Guilt gripped her. Everything seemed too hard this early in the day. She needed a shower, a mug of tea and something to dull the pounding behind her eyes.

'Going for a run?' she asked, in a vain attempt to move him away, to stop that questioning look searing her.

'Shortly. You joining me?'

'I should, I know, but…' She didn't have the energy. Plain and simple.

'Go have a shower and I'll put the kettle on for you before I go. You do look exhausted.'

His thoughtfulness only ramped up her guilt. He mightn't know for sure why she got so tired but he was prepared to help her out. 'Thank you.'

As she stripped off her nightgown and waited for the water to warm, she stared in the mirror, trying to see what Marshall might see when he looked at her. Nothing like the happy doctor he'd had a short fling with, that's for sure. Did he wonder where that woman had gone? He'd probably put the dark shadows staining her upper cheeks and the short and curly, easy-to-handle hair all down to motherhood.

Soaping the night's sweat off her skin, she smiled despite the weariness dragging at her muscles. Marshall looked as delectable as ever, as sexy as any hot-blooded woman could imagine. During the night, whenever she woke up, her thoughts immediately went to him, sleeping three rooms down from her.

The temptation to go and slip into bed with him was huge, but she managed to hold onto a thread of reason, knowing it was the wrong thing to do at this stage. They'd never get to talk and plan for the future if they went back to that steamy sex life that had produced Aimee in the first place.

But how long would she be able to hold out? What would she do if Marshall made a serious pass at her? Her body warmed at the thought of it, an ache of need centring at the apex of her legs.

It isn't going to happen, Charlie. It mustn't.

Sluicing the soap from her belly her hands paused over her hysterectomy scar. No more babies. That hurt. Hurt even more now that Marshall had come back into the picture. She didn't have the right to ask him to forego having more children.

Leaning her aching head against the glass wall of the shower, she fought the urge to have a damned good howl. Which only went to show how tired she was. She didn't do tears, remember?

Marshall watched the bathroom door close behind Charlie. Her feet were dragging this morning. What was with all this tiredness? Motherhood and a demanding career were obviously taking their toll on her, but he still had the feeling he was missing something. Like what?

He filled the kettle, got out the cereal she liked, sliced up some fruit into a small bowl, and set everything at her place at the table. He enjoyed doing little things for her. Made him feel as though he was contributing to the family. His family. Whether he lived with Charlie or not, he now had a family of his own. Aimee Hunter-Lang was his family and by association so was Charlie.

Goddamn, Charlie had stunned him when she'd shown him Aimee's birth certificate. His name had stood out. Hunter. Okay, Hunter-Lang, but he was more than happy with that. Thrilled, if the truth be known. He'd never planned on having kids. But he'd become a father without knowing it, without being hauled up to the line and made to decide, and, damn it—he liked it. That should surprise him, scare him away. But it didn't. Unfortunately. Because he really needed to put space between himself and those two females dominating his mind, his time and just about everything he did at the moment.

It was time to start talking to Charlie. Really talking. Because he might like it that he was a dad but nothing had changed. He still had to go away, might not be back for up to a year, and then only for a few days at a time. And Charlie needed to understand that.

A loud cry erupted from down the hallway in the vicinity of Aimee's room. 'Coming, my girl.' He grinned. His daughter didn't do delicate, or shy, or quiet. Everything about her was full on. Just like her dad. Like her mum had been.

'Morning, Marshall.' Brendon stood outside Aimee's room, looking from him to his granddaughter inside.

Guilt hit Marshall. Brendon probably did the morning routine with Aimee and since he'd arrived the guy hadn't got a look-in. 'I'll go and make you a coffee.'

'Don't be silly, lad. Your daughter wants up.' Brendon slapped his shoulder lightly as he passed him. 'I'm over wet nappies.'

Nappies. 'What's wrong with calling them diapers?' He grinned at this man who was so generous, not only with his home but with his heart.

He got an exaggerated eye-roll in reply.

Laughing, he went to swing Aimee out of the cot and kiss her on each cheek, blowing raspberries in between. The giggles she let rip were all the reward he required. Turning to head to the kitchen, he paused to scan the hundreds of photos covering one wall. Aimee, from the moment she'd been born to the present. Charlie had already put up one of him holding her.

'I'll add more of you soon.' Charlie leaned in the doorway, a small smile lightening those heavy eyes.

She reached up to kiss Aimee. 'Morning, sweetheart.' Tickling her tummy got more giggles.

The breath stuck in Marshall's throat. By the simple act of reaching out to her daughter Charlie had let go the front of her satin robe, exposing her cleavage and giving him a partial view of her beautiful breasts. Full, lush and damned tempting. His mouth dried. She might be tiny but she was perfectly endowed. He could remember the weight of her breasts in his hands, could hear the catch in her breath as he fingered her nipples, the groan escaping her lips as the desire built to an inferno inside her.

'Mum, mum.' Aimee kicked and wriggled, thankfully diverting his licentious thoughts back to more prosaic needs.

But her movements didn't cool his racing blood or knock down the instant hard-on the sight of those breasts had fuelled. Now what? He couldn't turn his back on Charlie, neither could he adjust his shorts to hide the bulge without drawing attention to himself.

The wriggling bundle in his arms was trying to get down. Bending, he placed Aimee carefully on the floor and said to Charlie, 'Your breakfast is ready. The tea might be getting cold.'

'Right. I'll get dressed. Oh…' Her gaze dropped to her front and she quickly pulled the robe closed over those thought-diverting breasts. 'I—I won't be long.'

He watched her cute butt as she all but ran to her bedroom. The satin slipped and slid, accentuating the curves that led to her legs. Legs he remembered waking up and finding entangled with his most mornings they'd been together. Always smooth, soft and yet firm, perfectly suntanned. Athletic. Sensational. Sexy as hell.

The groan that tore from his throat was filled with raw need. How long could he last without touching her, without feeling her naked body pressed against his? Without her sprawled across him after mind-numbing sex? How had he managed to stay in his own bed every night, knowing she was just down the hall?

So much for deflating his hard-on. It was bigger than ever. A cold shower might fix it. Or a solid, knee-slamming, gut-busting run. With a hard-on? Yes, damn it.

'Aimee, go and see Mummy. I'm going out.'

'Me come.'

'Not this time. Charlie,' he called, 'I'm heading out for a run. You okay with Aimee?'

'Sure.' And there she was, scooping Aimee up into her arms, avoiding looking at him. She'd dressed super-fast. Her blouse was skew, with the buttons lined up incorrectly. 'Let's have some breakfast, sweetheart. Morning, Dad.'

Brendon stood at the end of the hall. 'Morning, love.'

Great. Now he had to get out of the house without either of them noticing his predicament. He turned for the front door, in a hurry to get out of there.

As he closed the door he heard Brendon saying, 'I'm going fishing on Saturday on the Tongariro River, staying over for the night at Billy's shack.'

Up the ante, why don't you? Marshall's shoes

slapped the pavement as he headed for the lake. *Charlie and I alone in the house all damned night?* Knowing Brendon slept at the far end of the house had been about the only thing keeping him from knocking on Charlie's door most nights. He hadn't been able to bring himself to abuse the man's hospitality in that way.

He paused at the kerb, looked left, then right. Damn, got it wrong again. Looked right, then left and shot across the road to the path wending around the lake edge. The lake was calm this morning, as it often was until the afternoon breeze struck. At the far end, miles away, mountains rose into the pale blue of the morning sky. No denying the raw beauty of this place.

His heart ached. For the beauty. For Charlie. For the fact he had to leave at the end of next week. The army and his men awaited him.

Amazing. Charlie grinned. Once again Marshall had put her favourite breakfast together while she'd been in the shower after their run. He'd returned home with her this morning, not bothering with going further. 'I could get used to this.'

'Don't get your hopes up too high.' Dad grounded her fast.

'You don't think he'll come back to visit again?' Her heart sank. The truth was that she didn't either, but she couldn't help hoping. He was obviously still attracted to her. That had been monumentally obvious the other morning. But so far he hadn't acted on that attraction.

Dad buttered his toast. 'I'm sure he'll visit. Often.' The raspberry jam went on thickly. 'I just don't want you getting hurt. Marshall will do the right thing by you and Aimee. But I'm not sure that means making your breakfast every morning for the next fifty years.'

'You're talking commitment.' The cereal crunched between her teeth. 'I always knew that would be a difficulty, but I can't complain. I've got what I set out to find. If Marshall changes his mind about more involvement then that's a plus.'

Despite her tiredness, she suddenly felt free of all the worries of the last two years. Free of the need to try and make Marshall see things from her point of view. If commitment wasn't on his agenda, so be it. She'd find another way to make it work for Aimee. What that would be she didn't have a clue. But he was here for at least another week. Surely something would come to mind in that time.

Why had he come to see her? He hadn't known he had a child with her so it had to be because he'd had good memories of their time together. Had he thought they might pick up where they'd left off for a short while? A long, low sigh slipped over her bottom lip. Now, there was a thought. She'd love nothing more than to share a few hot nights under the sheet with him. But it wasn't going to happen.

She still had to tell Marshall about her dodgy health. It hung over her like a stormcloud. Swallowing the last of her breakfast, she pushed back from the table. Today was Friday, and then there was the weekend. Who knew what they might get to talk about then? But first she had a day of patients to see to. And tonight it was her turn to cook dinner.

At last. Charlie's car turned into the drive. She was well over an hour late home, which was unusual. Marshall's heart stopped its panicked beating and his brain deleted the horrific scenes he'd conjured up.

He opened her door and drank in the sight of her. 'Hey, you coming out to play?'

'Sure. I missed you at lunch. But I heard you were very busy with the boating-accident victims.'

'Yeah.' His grin vanished. 'When I was walking your way I saw a crowd on the beach and went to investigate. The moment I knew there were injured people out on the lake I volunteered to help. There were kids involved.' His voice hitched with anger. 'Two weren't wearing flotation jackets. How can parents be so careless?' He certainly wouldn't put Aimee's life at risk like that.

Charlie passed him a bag of groceries from the passenger seat before clambering out of the car. 'The national water safety council has an ongoing battle with that every summer. They swamp the television programmes with ads about wearing lifejackets, target the worst offenders, and yet our drowning statistics are appalling.'

Marshall nodded. 'This is very much a water-orientated country. I guess that explains some of the higher figures. But to let your kids out on a boat without any thought to their safety is beyond me. Why are people so careless with their kids' lives?' He shook his head at the stupidity of it.

'Which is why Aimee's already started swimming lessons and there's a miniature lifejacket hanging up in the shed alongside mine.' Charlie gave him a knowing grin. 'You're acting like a responsible dad.'

'I feel like one. How cool's that?' He grinned right back. Damn, but she was cute when she thought she'd bested him.

She changed the subject. Typical. 'Joseph says you were great out there today. Impressed the hell out of him.'

'Good to know. That's twice I've been able to help out. Seems I can be a doctor anywhere, not just on the battlefield.' He felt surprisingly good about that. Food for thought.

Her eye-roll was lopsided and made him laugh. Draping his free arm around her shoulders, he tugged her close. 'You and I are having a night out. All by ourselves. Dinner at Camper's. I believe they do a damned fine meal.'

She stumbled, quickly recovered. 'What about Aimee?' What happened to asking me?

'Brendon's happy to look after her. He's got to get his fishing tackle ready and cook a pie or something for lunch tomorrow.'

Her chuckle warmed him. 'Dad's fishing gear is always ready.'

'Yeah, I kind of figured that, but I'm not going to turn him down when he offers to baby-sit so I can take you out for some one-on-one time. So, my lovely, how about you take yourself inside for a long, relaxing shower or bath? Then dress in something gorgeous and we'll hit the town.' Excitement twirled in his belly. A night out with Charlie. Bring it on.

CHAPTER NINE

MARSHALL STARED AT the apparition floating down the hall towards him. A cloud of pink and yellow balanced on dangerously high heels. A hint of frangipani tickled his nose, bringing back memories of nights on the beach in Honolulu. The biggest, sweetest smile he'd ever seen split Charlie's face.

He could not speak. The roof could've fallen on his head and he wouldn't have got a word out. Charlotte was the most beautiful woman he'd ever seen, had ever had the good fortune to meet and touch, to kiss and laugh with. Holy Toledo.

'Marshall? Is something wrong?' The hesitancy in her voice mobilised him.

Two strides and he reached for her hands. Her fingers curled around his. 'No.' A swallow. 'Nothing.'

Her eyes scrunched up, her brow creased. 'I can change if my dress is all wrong. I'm so not used to dressing up these days.'

Now he got the hang of talking. 'Don't you dare. You look sensational. You took my breath away, that's all.' That's all? It was huge. He didn't usually stop breathing for anyone, let alone a woman. But Charlie was something else. If he ever fell in love it would have to be with someone exactly like her.

Relief battled with laughter in her eyes as she relaxed. 'Thank goodness for that. For a moment there I thought I'd have to wear my best pair of jeans.'

'Want to say goodnight to Aimee and your dad?' He had to get out of there, get Charlie to himself. He'd come to Taupo with the vague idea of spending time with her, and so he had, but he'd been sharing her all the time. Tonight was his. Theirs.

The waiter showed them to their table at the window, where they had a bird's-eye view of Huka Falls. Marshall had gone all out to find the best restaurant around. Charlie felt even more special, and determined to be fun and witty. And to stay awake—at least long enough to have dessert.

'This is lovely,' she murmured as she sank onto the chair he held out for her, having just nudged the waiter aside none too gently.

Then he further upset the young man by shifting his setting around so that he sat beside her and not opposite. 'I want to see the view too.'

The way his voice caressed her, she wondered exactly which view he meant. Though if he'd wanted to stare at her all night, he wouldn't have shifted, would he? Then his shoulder settled against hers and his hip touched hers and she smothered a sigh of pleasure. When his hand engulfed hers she smiled directly at him. 'Are we eating one-handed? Rice or mashed spuds maybe?'

His grin warmed her through and through. 'I've missed you. I want to be with you. It's been great staying at your house, getting to know you and your family, but tonight I want you for myself. All of you.'

Gulp. So they were to have an interesting, exciting evening, were they? Bring it on. Heat trickled along her veins, warming her from head to toe. She loved being treated like someone very special. It boosted her flagging ego, made her feel completely feminine again. 'I think I'll have a glass of champagne tonight.' Her strict regime of no alcohol could go to blazes. For tonight at least. She'd spent too long worrying about the possibilities of getting sick again. It was time to let her hair down and have fun.

Pity she didn't have that long hair Marshall had known before.

'Atta girl. Let's celebrate being together again after far too long apart.'

She could do that. And when a bottle of very good champagne appeared on their table almost immediately, she smiled. 'So you'd already ordered?'

'Yep. I remembered how much you used to enjoy drinking this stuff so hoped I could entice you into partaking tonight. I'm surprised that you don't drink wine at all now.'

So she couldn't relax completely. There was no way she'd spoil tonight with her sorry tale. 'The moment I suspected I was pregnant I gave up anything remotely alcoholic. Then I breast-fed Aimee for a while. Guess I've never really bothered since.' She raised her glass and toasted him. 'To you. Thanks for turning up out of the blue. You have no idea how much that meant.'

The rim of Marshall's glass tapped hers very carefully. 'The pleasure's all mine. I really had missed you and during this last deployment found myself thinking about you more and more. Besides, I wanted to know how your medical career was going since I had some input in it.' His lips seemed big and full against the delicate glass. Lips that could turn her body on with a single kiss. 'I'm glad I followed up on those instincts.'

'How often have you been deployed overseas since we were in Honolulu?'

'Twice.' When the gleam faded in his eyes she wished her question back. Marshall also had issues best left alone tonight.

Quickly changing the subject, she said, 'Tell me about your grandparents and their farm. Didn't you say you went there for school holidays?' It must've been the right thing to say because the tension she'd begun to feel in the hand holding hers backed off. She turned a little so she could watch all his facial expressions. There'd never be enough time just to absorb them, drink in this man who had her heart in his care.

'You'd have loved Grampy and Gran. They were so loving and sharing, like you and your father. I always put on a right performance when it was time to go back to whichever base my parents were at after my stays with them. I never understood why I couldn't just go to their local school.'

'So you went to a lot of schools?'

'Oh, yes. Too many. Not like you, eh?' His hand squeezed hers. 'What is it like, living in the same place all the time?'

That was easy. 'I don't know anything different. Apart from Mum's death, I had a truly happy childhood. I learned to sail on the lake and can catch a trout on a spinner.' She grinned when his eyebrows rose. 'There were week-long school trips to the mountains for skiing and day trips to Rotorua and the mud pools.'

'You sound like a travel brochure.'

The champagne bubbles burst on her tongue. 'That's divine. How could I have managed not to have this for two years?' She saw the waiter hovering and added, 'Guess we'd better order our meal.'

'What's the hurry?' Marshall picked up his menu.

I turn into a pumpkin at nine o'clock. 'I'm hungry.'

Charlie ordered steak, medium-rare, and mushrooms, while Marshall went for the lamb rack. 'Should try what this country's famous for.'

'Have you told any of your family about Aimee yet?' she asked quietly a little while later.

'No. I'd talk to you before I did that.'

She stared at him. 'You don't get it, do you?' Hadn't he picked up on any of her vibes? 'If I hadn't wanted you and your family's involvement with Aimee I would've sent you packing the moment you stepped through the front gate.'

As the waiter placed their meals before them Marshall kissed her cheek. 'Sometimes I get it wrong when it comes to knowing you.'

'We don't know much about each other at all.' But for her it had been love at first sight.

They talked and ate and enjoyed the wine for the next hour. Marshall was reticent about his army career and his parents. Charlie avoided her illness completely, fudging over those months when she'd been going through treatment. He raved on about the farm in Montana and how he'd learned to ride horses when he was nine. She spoke of her girlfriends and all the pranks they'd got up to as teenagers, and how she hoped Aimee would have such good friends as she grew up.

'Are any of those friends still living here?' he asked as he reached for the dessert menu.

'Jacqui's a teacher at the local high school, and Lisa is a radiologist up the road at Waikato Hospital. It's hard to see a lot of each other with our careers and families getting first dibs on our time. But twice a year we go away to a spa for a girls-only weekend.'

Marshall dropped his chin into his palm. He looked so sexy. Those come-to-bed eyes twinkled at her, making her toes curl with desire. How had she managed to stay out of his bed all week? 'Spare me. I can hear the three of you now, talking non-stop for the whole weekend.' Then he grinned at her. 'I'm having the strawberries. You?'

'Same,' she muttered around a sudden yawn. At least she'd made it until now for the first one. Hopefully she'd be okay for the rest of their meal. Shouldn't have had the champagne. Hurriedly covering her mouth as another yawn ripped through her, she forced herself to focus on the menu. 'Strong black coffee, too.'

Marshall squashed a flare of disappointment when Charlie yawned for a third time. They'd made it to nine o'clock before her tiredness had won out. He'd been hoping that a change of environment, a romantic dinner for two and just relaxing and talking might've kept her alert for longer. But seemed he was wrong. She was fading fast. Leaning close, he kissed her cheek. Then the corner of her sweet mouth. Then her lips. She tasted of champagne and mushrooms.

'Come on. Let's go home.' Standing, he lifted her up against him, kissing the top of her head softly. That exotic fragrance wove around him again. So Charlie. So erotic.

But Charlie sat back down. 'No. We've or-

dered dessert and coffee. I'd like to enjoy them.'
Her eyes were wide as she stared up at him, as
though she was deliberately holding them open
while her brain was trying to make her go to
sleep. 'Please.'

'Am I allowed to carry you out of here later?'
His grin was forced.

Glancing around the nearly full restaurant,
Charlie laughed. 'That'd be entertaining.'

'That's a yes, then.' He slid back onto his
chair and pulled it closer to her. To feel her thigh
against his gave him a sense of belonging. Yet
he never wanted to belong to someone, not even
Charlie. That would mean living with her whenever he wasn't on active duty, which he could
handle, even enjoy.

But he never wanted see the light go out in
her eyes as he packed to go away for months on
end. He knew the hurt and anger and sense of
abandonment that went with that look. Because
he'd felt it, seen it in his own eyes every time
his parents had headed out, leaving him behind.

Her elbow jogged him. 'Where have you
gone?' she asked as she tried to hide another
yawn.

'I'm right here, babe.' She shouldn't be so
tired all the time. About to ask about it, he
stopped, swallowed the words. They were hav-

ing a good time. Why spoil it? But he would be talking to her later. Maybe making an appointment for her with one of her partners at the medical centre.

Thankfully the desserts and coffee arrived and they went back to chatting about everyday things.

Marshall didn't have to carry Charlie out of the restaurant but he did carry her up the path and through the front door of her house. She was unbelievably light in his arms. Her eyelids had drooped shut, her eyelashes dark on her pale cheeks. Not even the light dusting of make-up had given colour to her face. With her head lolling against his shoulder, he felt incredibly protective of her. Wanted to look out for her. Knew he'd do anything to keep her safe. And happy. Anything except quitting the army and letting his men down. Even that was beginning to feel odd.

'Have a good time?' Brendon asked from the kitchen doorway. 'Charlie didn't make it all the way, then?' Sadness darkened his eyes as he followed them down the hall to Charlie's bedroom. 'Shame, when she was so excited about going out. It's been so long since she dated.' Ducking around them, he headed for the bed and pulled back the covers.

So Charlie hadn't been dating. Didn't make a lot of sense. She was attractive, gorgeous and very friendly. Having a toddler wouldn't prevent most hot-blooded men from wanting to spend time with her. 'We had a fabulous meal. Perfect setting for spending special time together.'

He placed Charlie on the bed, pulled up the sheet and tucked it under her chin. Standing back, he gazed down at the beautiful woman who'd somehow managed to snag his heart when he'd thought he'd had it well and truly locked away. Goddamn it, he loved her. No denying it. He loved her. For the way she just accepted him. For how she made no demands on him and didn't ask what he was going to do about his daughter. Love meant protecting. It meant making sure Charlie and Aimee got what was best for them.

Brendon cleared his throat. 'If it's all right with you, I thought I'd head away tonight. Bill and I like to be on the river before sun-up and he's already gone down to the shack.'

Twisting his head, he met the keen gaze of Charlie's dad. This man was on the same page as him. Wanted only the best for his daughter and granddaughter. And yet he was leaving Marshall alone with them for the weekend. Didn't he know what would most likely transpire? Then he saw the understanding, the acknowledgement of his daughter's needs in the man's eyes. 'Of course it's okay. Just bring me back a trout to taste, won't you?'

'Then I'll be off.' Brendon leaned down and kissed his daughter's cheek. 'Goodnight, sweetheart.' When he stood up he was blinking hard.

What the hell? 'Brendon?'

The guy turned for the hall, waving a hand over his shoulder. 'See you Sunday night.' Then the front door closed, and moments later Brendon's car pulled out onto the road, the sound of the engine fading into the night.

Marshall went through the house, locking up and turning off lights. Was Brendon afraid he was going to take his girls away to the States? The man's big heart wouldn't stop them going if that's what Charlie wanted, even though it would break him apart. If only the guy had said something, he'd have reassured him that wasn't going to happen.

He had no intention of bundling Charlie and Aimee up and dragging them off to another country where they knew no one and would be left to fend for themselves for months at a time. He might like the army but Charlie living on base? After growing up here with family and friends all around? It would never work. Not to mention being totally unfair.

He checked on Aimee and grinned to see her lying on her back with her teddy clutched tightly against her. How had he managed to father something so gorgeous that his heart hurt? She was a cracker of a kid. A Kiwi kid. He kind of liked that.

Now what? He was feeling antsy. His night had been cut short. There'd been no particular plans for after dinner but Charlie falling asleep on him hadn't featured either. His grin was self-deprecatory. So he'd been a boring date? Not if the way she'd cuddled in close to him had been a clue. That small, hot body had seemed to fold into his shape. No denying he'd hoped they might've got hotter than just touching.

It was time he found out what was going on with Charlie and why she had so little energy. He needed to know, wanted to help her if at all possible.

With a glass of bourbon in one hand and the bottle in the other, he returned to her bedroom and removed the workclothes she'd dumped earlier on the recliner chair in the corner. Pulling it out from the wall, he toed off his shoes and stretched out on the leather. The comfortable chair sucked him in, made him relax as he sipped his drink and watched over Charlie. He suspected he'd be there all night.

Not a problem. There'd been many nights in his life when he'd been on duty, watching out for something, someone. Tonight Charlie came under his scrutiny, and if she so much as whimpered in her sleep he'd be there for her. Not quite the way he'd thought he'd be spending nights with her when he'd hopped on that flight down to Auckland.

Strange how sitting here made him feel quite happy. True, he'd love nothing more than to slip into bed and make love to her, bring her to the peak of ecstasy and hear her cry out before entering her. But that hot and fast relationship they'd had two years ago had morphed into something that touched him more than physically. Talk about complicating things.

He sipped his drink and tried not to think about how he'd deal with this new feeling for Charlie when he flew out of the country.

Charlie rolled over. Sweat ran between her breasts. Her hand slid over her damp neck, then further down. Huh? She was still wearing her dress. Why hadn't she undressed before going to bed?

Sitting up, she pushed the sheet off and reached for the bedside light switch. A golden glow filled the dark room from the low-wattage bulb. The air in her lungs leaked out as she stared across at the nursing chair, where she'd spent many hours feeding Aimee. Correction, stared at the man sprawled over it. Marshall's long legs spread off the end; his arms hung on either side, with his hands brushing the carpet. And the cutest little snore ricocheted around the room.

Now she remembered—dinner. She'd fed strawberries to Marshall, one at a time. He'd licked her fingers every time he'd taken another berry, sending slicks of heat up her fingers, her arms and throughout her body, making her crave his touch. For a while she'd believed she was in heaven and that she'd manage to stay awake for a few more hours to enjoy what was so obviously going to be a very exciting night in Marshall's arms.

A rueful glance down at her dress. She'd let this wonderful man down. She remembered walking out of the restaurant clutching his arm, but the rest was a blank. No memory of the drive home, of coming inside or getting into bed. Marshall must've put her to bed. And now look at him. Sound asleep in her room. Had he been waiting, hoping she'd wake up so they could finish their evening in the way they'd been headed?

There was nothing to stop them having a good time now. A wicked sense of mischief teased her. Why not wake Marshall up and lead him to bed? Her bed. Or start undressing him, kissing any bare flesh that appeared. That would arouse him in more ways than one.

Carefully, quietly, she slipped out of bed and removed her dress. Thought briefly about pulling on a negligee, decided against it. The black lace panties and matching bra she wore were about as sexy as it was possible for her to get. The stretch marks on her breasts and belly gave her a moment of panic. The scar from her hysterectomy stood out, ugly against her pale skin. He'd notice, want an explanation. A sure passion-killer.

Tonight was not the time to tell him about that. A smear of make-up might help and she could turn the light off as soon as they were in bed.

Moments later she tiptoed across the room and knelt between Marshall's legs, her breath catching in her throat as she marvelled at his toned body. Even covered with a shirt and trousers, there was no denying the strength of his body or the very male bump shaping the front of his trousers. So close she only had to lean slightly one way or the other and she'd be touching him.

Her fingers were trembling as she reached for the buckle of his belt. She didn't want him to wake up immediately, would prefer to gradually undress him and enjoy each little exposure. Slowly, slowly she fed the end of the belt out of the buckle. Then started inching the zip down, one notch at a time over that bump. Her heart rate shot through the roof. Her fingers jerked the zip down the final centimetres. Desire raced along her veins, heating her rapidly all over, pooling at her centre.

She hadn't known this need, this feeling of urgency since Honolulu. Since this man had taken her to bed and taught her more about sex and loving than she'd believed possible. He'd woken her up in many ways, ruined her for any other man.

A sudden movement and her hand was pinned down. Marshall's hand gripped hers, his fingers splayed as he pressed his growing erection into her palm. His other hand grasped the back of her head and began to draw her close.

'Stop,' she croaked. And when he still pulled her closer she said loudly, 'Stop, Marshall.'

The hand on her head dropped away. The

other didn't. He tried to sit up but she was impeding him. Good. This was her show. They'd do things her way.

Looking up, she caught him watching her, eyes wide with lust, tongue tracking those full lips she loved to kiss. When he made to move again she shook her head and pushed him back into the chair. 'Wait.'

Returning her hands to his trousers, she finished unzipping them, all caution gone. She spread the opening wide and scooped into his boxers and lifted his weight into her palm, surrounded his hard length with her other hand. The throbbing erection felt like silk against her sliding fingers.

'Charlie. Oh, God.'

Leaning close, her mouth found him, her tongue licked and stroked, and the desire in her body ramped higher and higher until she shook with the need for him inside her.

His fingers wove through her hair, gripping as he held her head. His body strained in the chair, pushing up at her. His breathing was fast and hot, his thighs tense as he tightened them against her.

Then he reached for her shoulders and lifted her up. 'No, Charlie, you first.' The words were hoarse with need.

Scrambling to her feet, she tore her panties off and straddled him. As she hovered above him, her sex throbbing with need, she shook her head. 'No, Marshall. Together.'

He caught her waist. 'Condom. In my trouser pocket. Right side.'

So he *had* been hoping for this. She grinned and pushed into the pocket to find the small foil pack. Not that she'd get pregnant. He'd taught her to put one on with alacrity and finesse, and the moves came back in an instant. His passionate groan told her she'd got it right.

His hand found her wet centre, his fingers touched and caressed. She gritted her teeth, felt her neck cord as she fought to keep control, and reached for him again. This was their night. They had to share, to come at the same time. And then it was too late. She lost the battle as wave after wave of liquid need rocked through her, tightening her muscles and thrumming each and every nerve ending in her body.

She almost screamed. 'Marshall.'

His mouth quickly covered hers, took the next scream. His tongue danced with hers. Those lips held hers. And still she rocked with the power of her orgasm.

Slowly, slowly it dissipated and her heart rate returned to something resembling normal as she laid her head against his chest. 'You cheated,' she whispered.

'Lady, I never go first.' Then he pushed up against her, his penis finding her opening immediately.

Lowering herself onto him, Charlie met his thrusts as they became more urgent. Her hands gripped his shoulders as she rode him equally hard and fast. And his name filled the room as she came again. Their world closed around them as they found release, and then they were slumped together, their bodies melding into one another.

Finally, maybe hours later but most likely minutes, they both moved. Charlie lifted herself off Marshall. He caught her hand, tugged her back. His mouth covered hers with a kiss. A kiss that deepened until she thought she'd explode with need. Shaking, she pulled away. This time she tugged his hand and headed for her bed.

'Lady, any time you want to wake me up, feel free to go about it that exact same way.' Marshall climbed into bed and wrapped her in his arms.

'Any time, huh?' She grinned and reached to switch off the light.

He caught her hand, effectively stopping her.

'I want to look at you. It's been so long and my memories need a recharge.'

Huddling her shoulders, she snatched her hand back and tucked her arms under her breasts. Biting down on the flare of panic again clawing its way through her, she told him, 'I've got stretch marks now. I'd prefer you to remember me without those.' How lame could she get? He knew she didn't have hang-ups about her looks or body. But that had been then, this was now.

Beside her he leaned back against the headboard. 'Okay, Charlie. What's going on?' His tone was light and caring but there was steel running through it. There'd be no fobbing him off this time. 'Why do you always go to bed almost before the sun sets? Why did you all but fall asleep at the restaurant? Why don't you want me to see your beautiful body? I remember the Charlie who danced naked for me in my apartment.'

Here it was. The moment of truth. 'I...' Her mouth closed. She took a big breath and shuffled around so that she could see his face. She wanted to know exactly what he thought the moment he learned what had happened. She needed to know if he'd be around for Aimee. Now.

'I've had a hysterectomy.' His eyes widened. She held up her hand before he could say anything. 'I won't be having any more babies. Like you and I, Aimee's an only child.'

'Nothing wrong in that. I've managed without siblings. So have you.' His eyes bored into her. 'So why the operation? Something to do with Aimee's birth?'

If only. 'Eight weeks after Aimee was born I went for a routine check-up with my obstetrician and she discovered a growth on my womb. It was malignant.'

'Hell, Charlie.' Shock slammed into him, his face tightening, his eyes popping. 'Tell me you're okay now. Please.'

'As far as anyone can say, yes, my prognosis is good.' She shuddered. 'But sometimes I fear for the future. It's a black cloud hovering over me.'

'It must've been hell. Are you sure you're okay? You're not hiding anything from me?'

'I can show you the medical reports if that'll help.' But those hadn't taken all her fears away so she understood Marshall's need for reassurance.

'Oh, babe, I wish I'd known. I really do. You shouldn't have had to go through that on your own.' He reached for her, wrapped those strong arms around her and held on. 'I know Brendon was there, but…' His chin touched the top of her head. 'I don't know what I'd have done but I'd have been here for you.'

'I know you would've. That's why I kept looking for you.' She could stay tucked up in his arms for ever, feeling his strength, his tenderness, but they'd started this conversation. She wanted it finished.

Leaning back in his arms to see his face, she continued, 'My mum died of cervical cancer when I was seven. I was lucky. I have the greatest dad on the planet. He was always there for me as I grew up, and though I missed my mother I never felt lost or lonely. I'm sure I've disappointed him at times. When I came home pregnant he took that in his stride. My cancer was a huge shock for him, a rerun of when Mum got ill, but he's never once let me down.'

'In the short time I've been here I've seen how good he is, how strong his love is for you and Aimee.' Marshall straightened against the headboard, his eyes locking with hers. 'This is why you spent so much time trying to find me. If something goes wrong, you want the same for Aimee as you've had from Brendon.'

He saw straight to the truth every time. She didn't have to hit him over the head to make him understand. This was one of the things she loved about him. He could be brutally honest but he always got it. 'Yes. If anything happens to me, Aimee would need you in her life. She has to have one parent at least. Like I did. I need to know you'll look out for her.'

A cloud formed in his gaze. Setting her aside, he swung his legs over the edge of the bed and dropped his head in his hands. For a long time he said nothing, and she sat still, watching and waiting, knowing whatever he said wasn't going to be what she hoped for.

Finally he lifted his head and turned desperate eyes on her. 'I hear you. I even understand you. But, Charlie, I'm nothing like Brendon. It's not in my make-up.'

Talk about brutally honest. Her heart sank. He'd hinted at his past and she'd wondered if that might affect how he'd react to this situation. But to not even think about it beyond a few minutes—which surely hadn't given him time to think of the whole situation, not just his part in it—bowled her flat. 'You've been fantastic with Aimee all week. Playing with her, dressing and feeding her, being endlessly patient. Yet now you're pulling back from a chance to see if we can make it work.'

Standing, he crossed the room, flicked the

curtain open and raised the window so he could lean out, his arms braced wide, his head bowed. 'I had a hard upbringing. Dad ruled with his fists. What if I'm the same?'

'Have you ever hit anyone?' She reckoned she knew the answer already.

'No.'

Exactly. 'You're a strong, tough man, Marshall, but you're not a hard one. Nothing's changed. I would trust you with Aimee any day.'

His shoulders stiffened, his back straightened and he turned to look at her. 'Thank you.' His gaze locked with hers and it was as though he was searching right inside her. Then, 'Did you ever want to find me for us? Or was it all about our child?'

Her heart slowed. Where was this going? 'I watched you walk away in Honolulu and I ached from the need to chase you down the road to beg you to stay in touch, to come and see me when you had the time.' She swallowed around a lump that suddenly clogged her throat.

'I knew you didn't want any long-term relationship but I'd have sold my soul to have another week with you. A month even.' Her gaze remained fixed on him. 'So, yes, I wanted to find you. For me. For us. And, heaven knows,

I tried. Even when I suspected you'd be angry if I did make contact.'

'I'd never be angry with you.'

'You confused me by leaving your email address in my pocket and then having my emails bounce back.'

'At the time I believed you were better off without me. I still do.' Marshall slowly leaned back against the window ledge, folded his arms across that expansive chest. 'But…' He paused. 'Those weeks were something special, weren't they? Wild and crazy, fun and exciting. Yeah, very special.'

'Is that why you came to see me?'

'I haven't been able to get you out of my head. It's like we haven't finished what we started. At the end of my last posting I headed home thinking I'd be able to put you into perspective once I was in familiar surroundings and no longer trying to distract myself as I listened to gunfire in the middle of the night.'

'Didn't work, huh?' She tried for a smile, failed badly. 'So you came for another fling. Or a continuation of the old one.' The bitterness in her voice disgusted her. She didn't usually act like this, yet her tongue was like a runaway train. 'I'm surprised you stayed when you learned I had a child. Hardly the excitement you were looking for.'

Crossing the room, he gripped her elbows and hauled her up off the bed to hold her as his eyes poured out his anger and his hurt. 'Stop it, Charlie. I don't deserve that any more than you deserve what's happened to you. I got a shock when I realised Aimee was mine. Who wouldn't? But I stayed. I'm still here. And I'll always be in contact. For Aimee. For you. No matter what the future brings. That's my promise to you.'

Then he kissed her. Hungrily. As though he hadn't had a woman for a very long time. As if he'd been waiting for her and the sex they'd just shared hadn't even begun to fill a void within him. His hands slid over her arms, over her back, her tummy, cupped her breasts.

Pulling her mouth away from his demanding lips, she murmured, 'I'm sorry. That was selfish of me.' When he leaned close again she put a finger on his lips. 'I like the fact you'll stay in touch. Hopefully, my health will keep improving and we won't need to revisit this discussion.' Then she returned to kissing him. She could give him time to take in this latest information. Her heart might be squeezing with anguish at the thought of Marshall leaving but that was nothing new.

As her body cried out its need for his she gave herself up to the moment. Plenty of time to deal with the debilitating pain of letting him go after he'd gone.

CHAPTER TEN

CHARLIE SAT ON the veranda, overseeing Aimee playing in her paddling pool. At the barbecue Marshall was cleaning up after the lunch he'd cooked for them.

'What are you smiling about?' He dumped dirty paper towels in the rubbish bin.

'Just thinking how this time last week Dad told me to stop searching for you and see what the universe brought.' Her smile widened. 'Weird.'

'A troop carrier brought me, not the universe.' He parked his delectable butt on the top step and tipped his head back to look up at her. 'But, hey, who's checking?'

'I promise not to watch the sky too often after you've gone.' She kept the smile on her face despite the sadness threatening to break through.

His big hand covered her knee. 'I've put all my contact addresses and numbers on your laptop, as you asked. Feel free to call or email any time. I will answer. Might be late if we're out on patrol, but I'll get to it as soon as possible.'

'Thanks.' It was good to know he'd be contactable. Which had been all she'd wanted—at first. Now, having admitted she loved Marshall, she wished for so much more. But did she really want him here with her if his heart was elsewhere? Yes. No. Not really. She had six days left to enjoy his company. Why waste them being miserable? 'Shall we take a picnic tea out to Acaia Bay later?'

The hand on her knee squeezed lightly and his eyes lit up. 'Sounds like a good idea.' Glancing across at Aimee, he grimaced. 'She seems full of energy this afternoon. More than usual. Must know I've got plans for her mother when she goes to sleep.'

An afternoon in the sack with Marshall. She couldn't think of a better way to spend the hours. Except Aimee was busy jumping up and down, intent on making the biggest splashes possible. 'Funny how she seems to know when I want her to go down on time.'

'If not energy then she'll run out of water shortly.' Marshall grinned and leaned up on his elbow to kiss her. 'I could put a wee hole in the bottom of the pool to hurry things up.'

Her elbow caught him in the shoulder. 'Shame on you, Marshall Hunter.'

The sound of car doors banging reached her from the other side of the fence. Please, don't be coming here. Not that she was expecting anyone. Then the gate opened and four people streamed through. 'Keisha and Toby.' And their boys. She shivered. The afternoon had just turned grey.

'The woman you mentioned with the breast lump?' Marshall stood and held his hand out to her.

'Yes. Can't say I'm too surprised. If I'd got that message I'd want to know what's going on. But it's not going to be easy.' Letting him tug her to her feet, she stepped down to greet the couple trudging up her path. 'Hey, you're home.' She stated the obvious, letting them set the tone for the meeting.

'Got into Auckland last night and drove down today.' Toby stood irresolute, one arm around Keisha's waist. 'I'm sorry we've barged in but…' His voice petered out.

Reaching a hand out to Keisha, who stood like a rabbit caught in headlights, Charlie said, 'It's okay. I understand what you're going through.' More than most.

Keisha gripped her hard, nearly breaking the

bones in her fingers. 'Is it...?' Swallow. 'Does this mean I've got...?' Another swallow. The word was hard to say, and Charlie knew that once Keisha did utter it then it became all too real.

Charlie looked directly at Keisha. 'We don't know what your mammogram means yet. Come inside and we'll talk.'

Marshall stepped up beside her. Held his hand out to Toby. 'I'm Marshall Hunter, Charlie's friend. Want me to keep your boys occupied while you talk with Charlie? There's a football in the shed.'

Toby shook his hand in return. 'Would you? That's good of you. Calib, Zac, this is Mr Hunter. You're to go with him while Mum and I talk to Dr Lang, okay.'

'Sure,' Calib answered. 'Can Aimee play, too?'

Giving Marshall a grateful peck on the chin, Charlie whispered, 'Thank you. I owe you.'

'We'll make up for lost time tonight,' he whispered back, and planted a big kiss on her lips. No subtlety, then.

Turning to the upset couple, she indicated that they follow her inside. Keisha's eyes were on stalks as she agreed. Once inside she gasped, 'Is he really just a friend? That'd be a waste.'

So much for doctor-patient boundaries. Sometimes Taupo seemed even smaller than it actually was. She understood Keisha was deliberately delaying the conversation to come. So, 'Marshall is Aimee's father.' No secret there. The man had made sure everyone at the medical centre knew, which meant hundreds of others were now aware of the fact, too. 'I'll make some coffee.'

She filled the coffee percolator and sat her guests down at the table. 'How was Phuket? You've all got great suntans.'

Keisha answered. 'We had a fabulous time. Right up until the moment we got home and heard the messages.' She seemed stunned and yet simultaneously thinking about many things.

Toby added, 'We had to come see you. No way could we wait until Monday.'

'It's truly all right,' she tried to reassure the distressed couple, at the same time knowing exactly what they were going through. The shock, the fear and the many unanswerable questions. All very debilitating. Dropping onto a chair, she placed her elbows on the table and her chin in her hands. 'Keisha, your mammogram shows an abnormality. There's a dense spot in your breast, like a lump. At the moment no one can say for sure what it is.'

The other woman's face whitened. Toby took her hand and held on tight. Suspecting and knowing were miles apart. And at this point they hadn't had confirmation that Keisha did have cancer.

Charlie continued quietly, 'The radiology centre has left you a message, too.'

Keisha nodded. 'I have to make an appointment for another mammogram. She said something about the X-rays of one breast not being very clear.'

'That's standard practice. The woman phoning is not a doctor so can't tell you anything about your X-ray results.' The coffee percolator made sucking sounds and she got up to turn it off. 'Considering you were away, I thought it best we make you an appointment. Eleven o'clock on Monday. You can change the time if that doesn't suit.'

'We'll be there,' Toby growled.

'The radiologist will give you an ultrasound scan. He'll also take a tiny sample from the lump to send to the laboratory. Until he gets the results of that there's nothing you can do.'

'Except worry ourselves sick.' Keisha leaned against her husband, her fingers now interlaced tightly in her lap. 'How long will it take for the results to come back?'

'A few days. I won't deny that'll be hard.' Absolutely terrifying, if the truth be known. They wouldn't get much sleep over those days. 'If you want to talk about anything in that time, phone me. Or drop in. I really don't mind.'

Gleeful shouts had them all turning to look out the window. Marshall had the boys kicking the ball at one end of the lawn while Aimee tottered around them in her wet swimsuit, laughing and chasing the ball.

'He's good with kids, your man,' Toby said.

'It's all very new to him, this fatherhood stuff.' He'd taken to Aimee like cheese to crackers. But try telling Marshall that.

Keisha watched them, her hungry gaze flicking from Calib to Zac, Calib to Zac. Tears gathered in her eyes. 'My boys. Will they be all right? If…?'

'Don't go there.' Yeah, right. Like she hadn't? The moment she'd heard she had to have tests done she'd panicked and had spent every waking hour—which had been most of the days and nights leading up to getting her results—making numerous and varied plans for Aimee if the worst happened.

Keisha turned big, sorrow-filled eyes on her. 'Yeah, right,' she echoed unwittingly. 'How did you manage…' she wiggled her fingers in the air '…not to go there?'

'I didn't. It's a very scary time.' The not knowing had eaten away at her, as it did with anyone facing the same horrendous situation. 'I suggest you try to take things one day at a time. You couldn't have got an appointment any sooner. The lab will do their best to have answers quickly. They always do in these cases.'

'I have to say it, Charlie.' The woman drew a deep breath and spat it out. 'Cancer.'

Toby blanched at his wife's sudden directness. 'Keisha, sweetheart…'

'No, Toby, I'm saying it as it is. I have to. At the moment that's what we're looking at. This time next week we might be dancing in the street and celebrating a good result.' Her voice lowered. 'Or I might be baking and filling the freezer with meals for you to give the boys while I'm in hospital.'

Charlie dredged up a smile. 'Why do women always start trying to sort out their family in times like this? That seems to be their first concern.'

'Guess it's the nurturing instinct in us.' Her bottom lip trembled and Charlie reached across to squeeze her hand. Nothing she could say would make this go away.

Then a loud shriek from outside had Charlie leaping out of her chair. 'Aimee?' Loud sobs followed that she recognised as Aimee hurting, intermingled with a deep male voice talking lovingly.

'Sorry, but I've got to go and see to Aimee.'

Toby's words stopped her. 'But Aimee's dad's with her.'

'He isn't used to comforting her when she's hurt or upset.'

'Give him a moment. Seems to me he's doing his best.' Toby stared her down. 'Come on, Doc, let him show Aimee who he is to her.'

Slowly she inched back down onto the chair. 'You're right. But I want to be there for Aimee.'

Keisha nodded. 'That nurturing thing. But Toby's right. If Marshall hasn't had much to do with kids, and especially with his daughter, then he's doing really well. It's gone quiet out there.'

Charlie blinked. 'So it has.' Pride swelled in her chest. Marshall was a fantastic dad. If only she could get him to see that, to believe it.

Marshall watched Toby gently help Keisha into the car and close the door with a soft click. 'Poor bastard. He doesn't have a clue what to do other than be right beside his wife every moment.'

Charlie grimaced. 'Not much either of them

can do right now. The waiting is horrible.
They'll be wondering if Keisha is going to die,
if she'll live and see her boys grow up, if she
even has cancer or not. They'll make plans for
the boys in case the worst happens and then
change them every five minutes.'

His heart thudded in his chest. Charlie was
speaking from experience. If only he hadn't
changed his email address he'd have been here
for her. Yeah—if the army had given him leave.
'How long did you have to wait to find out your
results?'

'Ten days. Felt like ten years. I hardly slept
that whole time. Spent hours just watching
Aimee in her basinet, drinking in as much about
her as possible. She was so tiny and vulnerable
and I didn't know how long I'd be there for her.'
Her voice caught and she slapped the back of
her hand over her cheek.

Wrapping an arm around her shoulders, he
hauled her up against him. 'But you are here,
and the future's looking good. Aimee's happy,
and lucky to have the best mom ever.' He kissed
the top of her head. 'You made it, Charlie. Hang
onto that and try to let the past go.'

She sniffed against his shirt. 'I'm trying, believe me. But having to tell Keisha she might
have cancer threw me. I thought I'd manage

but it seems I haven't completely put it all behind me.'

'You're strong and getting stronger by the day.' He put her away from him enough to be able to see her face. 'Promise to let me know any time you feel you can't manage. I can't make up for not knowing but I can be sure to talk with you any time you're worried. Okay?'

Her teeth left an indentation on her bottom lip as she nodded. 'Okay. That would be good.' She didn't look overly convinced, though.

Hours later Marshall tucked a strand of Charlie's hair behind her ear as she slept, curled up against him in her bed. He hadn't had more than a catnap through the night, afraid to miss any moment holding Charlie to him. What she'd told him about her cancer had cut him deep. How had she coped with all the worry and fear it had brought while trying to look after a baby? At least she'd had Brendon but Keisha was way better off having Toby with her at this time.

His hand fisted. If only he'd known. If only he hadn't deleted his address. If only a whole bunch of things. But nothing could be changed except what he did for the future. He had to stay in touch with Charlie, no matter what.

Seeing the first hint of sunlight creeping

around the edge of the curtains, he grimaced. Friday. Tomorrow—well, tomorrow was his last day here.

He'd spent as much time as he could with Aimee during the past two weeks, which had been pretty much all of it. Being with Charlie hadn't come as easily. She had a job to do. She'd pointed out that asking for time off when she'd already taken months over the previous year and a half didn't sit easily with her.

The reason for that time off terrified him. Was Charlie really going to make it? She had to. No argument. Aimee needed her. It was sad that there'd be no siblings for his girl but not the worst thing to come out of this. Charlie had all the love she needed from her father and it would be similar for Aimee. But cancer? Showed how little he had to do with everyday medicine if he hadn't recognised her gauntness and lack of energy for what it was. He still didn't want to think about Charlie and cancer in the same sentence. But there'd be plenty of nights ahead when he wouldn't be able to avoid it.

Since learning what was behind her exhaustion, he'd wanted to do even more for her. But mostly, every night when she'd crawled into bed, exhausted as usual, he'd followed and held her as she'd fallen into that first deep sleep. He'd lain awake, hearing every breath she'd taken, feeling the rise and fall of her breasts against his arm, absorbing her warmth and scent. Trying to pass his strength on to her.

About an hour later she'd wake up suddenly, her eyes wide and excited, her lips searching for his mouth, her hand pushing down his body until she encountered the hard result of him holding her so close.

They'd made love, sometimes so slowly and exquisitely it hurt him inside where his heart lay. At other times their passion and need had driven them wild with excitement and they'd had to restrain themselves from crying out loud enough to be heard throughout the house.

Afterwards Charlie usually fell back into such a deep sleep it was as though she was unconscious, and he'd return to holding her. He loved her more and more every day. Falling asleep and missing a single moment of Charlie in his arms was not possible. Time was precious—and running out fast.

His ticket for his flight out of Auckland on Saturday night was tucked out of sight in a pocket of his pack but hiding it hadn't changed the fact. He was leaving. Going back to the States. And the army. Walking away from this wonderful, gutsy woman. Leaving his daughter behind because this was the best place for her. The days were jerking along, sometimes whizzing by, sometimes crawling so slowly he had to keep checking his watch to make sure he hadn't got the time wrong.

The slow times were when Charlie wasn't with him. At times he resented her patients and then hated himself for that selfish emotion. She was doing one hell of a balancing act, juggling Aimee's needs, her patients' requirements, her father and him. All while she was so goddamned exhausted. Yet every night she went to bed with a wicked gleam in those deep blue eyes. Every morning she woke up with enthusiasm and laughter on her lips.

No doubt about it. He would miss her like crazy. So much for coming and working her out of his system. She'd managed to completely infiltrate every cell of his body. She would never leave him in peace now. Even when he was halfway round the world in some alien place, putting broken soldiers back together in the makeshift hospitals they used.

Charlie would be his guardian angel, there to escape to in the middle of the night when he couldn't sleep for thinking about the next day's duties.

Maybe that was a load of crap and he just had

to accept he loved her but wasn't going to do a damned thing about it for fear of hurting her.

Saturday. Charlie stared at the dent left by Marshall's head on the pillow beside hers. He'd made love to her as the sun had come up. Tender, yet gripping love that had spoken of the things he couldn't say to her. He did care about her, maybe came close to loving her. She'd felt that in his touches, his kisses, the times they'd spent talking, or when they'd just sat watching their daughter.

He was leaving her.

When he'd climbed out of bed to go for a run there had been tears in his eyes. She'd reached for him but he'd avoided her outstretched fingers. 'If I get back into bed with you, chances are I'll never leave.'

Yeah, well, what was wrong with that? Her heart squeezed with need as he slipped out of the room. Honest to a fault, he'd never hidden the fact he couldn't stay. Tears slid from the corners of her eyes and tracked down to her ears, on further to soak into her pillow. She let them come, though she should be fighting them. She'd allow herself this one moment of self-pity then she'd get up and go on with her life.

But first she had to get through the remainder

of the day until Marshall hopped into his rental vehicle and drove away. Smudging tears across her face, she sat up. There were two ways to do this. She could go around with a dark heart all day and make everyone miserable, and probably make Marshall glad to be escaping.

Or they could celebrate the fact they'd found each other again and that Aimee now had her father in her life, albeit mostly via the ether.

She tossed the sheet off and her feet hit the floor. Pulling a drawer open, she chose a top with shoestring straps in a sky-blue colour that highlighted her eyes. From her wardrobe she took a short denim skirt that emphasised her slim legs and hugged the curves of her backside. A black G-string and a very lacy push-up bra went onto the bed beside the other clothes. Marshall might not get to see the underwear but she'd feel more feminine for wearing it. And he'd certainly get an eyeful of what he was leaving behind when she waltzed out to the kitchen dressed in that skirt and top. She wasn't going down without a fight.

She got the eyeful bit right. Marshall was leaning against the bench, pouring water down his gasping throat, when she hit the kitchen nearly an hour later, her hair washed and styled, her face lightly made up. He spluttered water down the front of his tee shirt and his eyes bugged out. Coughing and wiping his mouth with the back of his hand, he stared at her.

Then his mouth lifted into a grin and his eyes filled with a wicked gleam. 'Hey, Charlie, you look fabulous. You've gone all out this morning.'

So he'd caught onto her ploy. Good. At least he'd remember her as a sexy woman and not just a tired mother and doctor. 'Thought we'd have the full works this morning. A brunch rather than breakfast. Bacon, eggs, sausages, mushrooms, tomatoes.'

Dad walked in as she was talking. 'We could pop a bottle of bubbles, too. There's one in the other fridge.'

She wasn't celebrating Marshall leaving. But, then again, she was going all out to make a lasting memory. 'Great idea, Dad. I'll chop up the peaches, apricots, strawberries and raspberries I got at the roadside stall yesterday for a fruit salad.'

Marshall continued leaning against the bench. His legs not capable of holding him up any more? Had she finally knocked the stuffing out of him? He did look a bit stunned. Had expected her to stand around sniffling all day, had he? She had news for him. She wasn't going to show him how much this hurt. That would come later, in the middle of the night when he filled her head and prevented her from sleeping.

Nudging Marshall in the waist, she reached for the kettle. 'Out of the way, big boy. I've got heaps to do and I can't start without that first cup of tea inside me.'

His legs did work. Just. He stumbled sideways, leaned against the stove. 'Ah, right. What can I do to help with this banquet?'

Dad beat her to answering. 'Get out of those shorts and shirt first. Then there's Aimee to see to. Later you can help me cook this mountain of food on the barbecue.' His voice went up a notch and he looked away, but not before she saw the distress in his eyes.

She nearly canned the whole idea right then. They might be fooling themselves they were going to have a blast today, but everyone was hurting. But as she opened her mouth, Marshall spoke.

'Sounds like we've got ourselves a plan. Thanks, both of you.' And he disappeared quick-smart out of the room.

Charlie stared after him until Dad draped an arm over her shoulders. 'He's no happier than you, my girl.'

'So why go?'

'He belongs to the army. Not us.' His hand squeezed her arm gently before he stepped away.

Dad's understanding got in the way of her determination not to let her emotions go on the rampage. Sniffing hard, she made the tea, squeezing the teabag until it nearly split, stirring in the milk until liquid spun over the side of the mug. Sniff, sniff. Clang. The teaspoon hit the bottom of the sink.

'Mummy, I got up.' Aimee wrapped her arms around Charlie's knees.

'Hey.' Reaching down, she lifted up her baby. 'How did you get up all by yourself? Bet Daddy helped you.'

'I caught her climbing out of the cot.' Marshall grinned from the doorway, his eyes full of pride. 'You're going to have to put her in a bed any day now, little monkey that she is.'

Hugging Aimee tightly, Charlie managed a smile for him. 'Wonder where she gets that from.'

'Don't look at me. No monkeys in my family. Until now.' And once again he headed away, this time hopefully going to the bathroom.

Once again Marshall found himself clearing up after the barbecue. It had become his job since he'd arrived. It was almost as if, by having allocated jobs, it meant he had a place in this family. Something new for him. Different from being ordered to do something in the army. Or in his parents' house. This was about sharing the chores and doing things for those he cared about. And who cared about him.

Charlie was putting Aimee down for her afternoon nap. He'd held his girl on his knees throughout brunch, had kicked a ball around the yard with her afterwards, with Charlie egging them on from the sidelines, and he'd kissed her goodbye. His heart had come near to breaking then. But going away was the right thing to do. One day Aimee—and Charlie—would thank him for this. One day they'd understand. He hoped. Because right now he sure as hell didn't.

One-thirty. Nearly time to hit the road. Brendon had gone into his shed a few minutes ago. He'd go and see the guy, try to let him know how much he meant to him.

Brendon stood at his workbench, viciously sandpapering a wooden table. Marshall wondered if the older man was mentally attacking him as he worked.

Clearing his throat, he spoke above the rasping sound of Brendon's work. 'I want to thank you for everything you've done for me. Especially for the way you've welcomed me into your home.'

The sanding continued as the fingers gripping the sanding block whitened. 'You're welcome. Any time.'

In other words, he was meant to come back. Swallowing the sour taste in his mouth, he continued. 'I truly appreciate that.' Not that he'd be back in a hurry. He'd decided that would only complicate things and give Charlie reason to hope for more from him.

The sanding block clunked down on the bench and Brendon clapped the dust off his hands. 'Right.' He glanced around the shed's interior, his gaze finally settling on a small catamaran stashed in a corner, cobwebs attaching the yacht to the wall. 'I caught her struggling to haul that outside a couple of months ago, adamant she was going sailing.'

'It's chained to a peg in the floor.' He'd known they'd end up talking about Charlie. Unavoidable.

'Broke my heart to see her unable to do something that a couple of years ago was easier than falling off a bike for her.' Brendon's voice sounded hollow. 'I chained the damned thing up so she couldn't try again.' His head rolled from side to side. 'My girl used to be so strong.'

And you're afraid she won't ever regain that strength.

He wouldn't even think about that. 'I see her as very strong mentally. She never wavers. Always looking out for Aimee, her patients. Refuses to let the cancer set her back.' If it dared to come back it was in for a hell of a battle from Charlie.

'You are right, lad. She is strong. I only hope she's strong *enough*. The next weeks are going to be hard for her.'

A perfect shot. Straight at his heart. Marshall winced. Couldn't blame the man for putting his daughter's case. 'I have to go, Brendon. There is no other option.'

'Keep moving? That the army way, lad? Or your way?'

'It's the only way I know how to live, how to be me.' Except now that way of life seemed odd from where he stood.

From the doorway came, 'That's a copout.' Charlie's hands were firmly on her hips. 'You fall back on that excuse for everything. You've been conditioned to think like that. Yes, it is the army way. No, you don't have to live like that. You can make a life that suits you and get what you want from it.'

'Maybe I have.' The path of least resistance.

Yeah, even he could see that. 'But there is no getting away from the fact that I have to follow orders, which means going wherever I'm told.' He could tell the army to stick the next contract due to be signed in a few weeks, but then what? Could he become a GP in a small town? He'd still be helping people, caring for their families.

Brendon slipped past Charlie and headed outside. No fond farewell, then. He couldn't blame the guy. He was hurting his girl.

Charlie came inside and approached him, her eyes brimming with need, love and earnestness. 'Well, here's my way. I love you, Marshall. I love you with all my heart and then some. Have done since that first day in the ED when you teased me about my funny accent.' She stepped close, rose up on her toes and kissed him hard on the mouth.

His arms rose almost of their own volition to wrap around her. Pushing his tongue between her lips, he tasted her mouth, felt his knees weaken. God, it would be so easy to stay. To pretend he didn't have commitments elsewhere. To pretend it would all work out—that he'd be a great dad, a wonderful husband and turn into a settled doctor living in small-town New Zealand.

It took every last ounce of his strength to put

Charlie aside. 'Nothing's going to change because of what you've revealed, Charlie. I still won't be around for you.'

Her eyes glittered with anger. 'Don't you get it yet? Having you some of the time is better than never. Loving you means letting you be the person you are, not trying to change you into someone else, not tying you down in one place. I understand that would be the quickest way to turn our relationship sour.'

Tempting. So bloody tempting. To stop in one place occasionally. To have special time out with Charlie and Aimee, to be the partner and parent and still have his army career with the duty that was his rod.

So damned unfair on them. He could see it now. Aimee crying every time he left, begging him to stay one more night, to take her to school the next day. It would be him all over again. Except he'd be the one going away.

Air hissed through his teeth. 'You deserve better than that. You can and should have the whole enchilada. So should Aimee. I'm going home, Charlie.' Home? A cold, lonely barrack room. Home.

'Sure.' Her hurt blinked out at him, cutting him to the heart.

He continued relentlessly, trying to ignore the

pain in her face that reflected what crunched inside him. 'You need to find a good, kind man who'll love and cherish you, who'll come home to you at the end of the day and sit down with a glass of wine to talk about what you've done. A man who'll take Aimee to school sports.'

The colour drained from Charlie's cheeks at that reminder of what she'd wanted for him. He had to make her see he was right. 'A man who'll take you on vacation, be there to teach Aimee things. A man totally unlike me.' His lungs were struggling to inhale. His blood had slowed to the point he was in danger of collapsing.

He wanted to haul her into his arms and tell her he'd made a mistake, that he didn't mean a word of it and that he'd stay. Except he knew himself too well, knew he couldn't. So he wasn't finished. 'Find yourself a man who'll see you into old age, Charlie.'

Her voice sounded like it came through a gag. Her eyes leaked tears. But her shoulders were drawn back tight and her chin pointed at him. 'You're wrong, Marshall. I don't need anyone to take care of me. What my heart needs is you as and when I can have you. Nothing more, nothing less.'

Reaching his hands to her shoulders, he felt the tension in her muscles, the tremors racking her body. Leaning down, he kissed her forehead then her lips. 'Take care, Charlie.' *Goodbye, my love*. And he strode away with a resolution he didn't feel.

Hamilton. The road sign indicated to continue straight ahead.

Auckland. Turn right to bypass the city.

Marshall blinked. 'Here already?' He hadn't noticed a thing as he'd driven up from Taupo, his mind firmly fixed back with two beautiful females.

Indicating to turn right, he turned onto the road leading to Auckland and his trip back Stateside. No stopping today, no turning around and going back to Charlie.

He swallowed hard, trying to dislodge the blockage in his throat. Failed miserably. The vehicle surged forward until he lifted his foot from the accelerator. 'Careful. Trying to outrun that love and sadness in Charlie's eyes isn't going to work. She's a part of you for ever, Marshall.'

Yeah, maybe, but that didn't mean he had to put her heart in jeopardy. He loved her beyond reason but how did he know that love would last through everything life tossed up? Could he guarantee he'd always be there for Charlie in heart and mind, if not in body? No, he couldn't.

Despite the sense of belonging to her family that had quickly overtaken him these past weeks, it scared him to think they'd rely on him to always come through for them.

He'd failed Rod, hadn't he? Rod had been the closest thing to a brother he'd ever had. The pain and guilt over losing him hadn't diminished at all.

He turned onto the motorway. The international airport was getting closer by the second.

Charlie had been through enough. He couldn't ask her to face more heartache. And he couldn't expect his little girl to get to know him and then face the devastation of losing him, like Rod's kids had.

Those two boys had been completely lost and bewildered as they'd waited for Daddy to come home from yet another mission. It had taken a long time for them to finally understand that Rod was never coming home. And it had thrown them completely. Karen had told him how little Johnny wet the bed every night while his older brother had taken to lashing out at his friends at school. Only now was counselling starting to show some signs of working to improve the situation.

He didn't want that for Aimee.

Or Charlie. There were no guarantees with his life in the army. End of.

His heart clenched so hard he feared he was having a cardiac event. He was, just not a medical one. Pulling to the side of the road, he opened the door and dragged in a lungful of fresh air, waited for the pain to ebb. Knew it would never, ever go away completely.

CHAPTER ELEVEN

THREE WEEKS LATER Charlie clicked onto patient files prior to seeing her first patient for the day. Notes from Keisha's surgeon caught her attention. Keisha had had a full mastectomy. Treatment would start in six weeks' time. Concern slipped under Charlie's skin, raised the hairs on the back of her neck.

She'd hoped fervently that this wouldn't be the case. An image of those two beautiful boys kicking a ball around the front lawn with Marshall sneaked into her head. Aged seven and eight, they were so young to be facing this. Some kids didn't get a fair shot at childhood.

Like Aimee. She mightn't have known what had been going on with her mother but she'd missed out on lots. The breastfeeding had stopped. There'd been many nights when her grandfather had put her to bed because her mother had been too ill to do something so simple and vital. Charlie sighed.

Aimee didn't appear any the worse for her rocky start in life. She had yet to meet a happier, more well-adjusted little girl. Whether that was due to Aimee's nature or her loving grandfather, Charlie didn't know but she was very grateful. And now, with Marshall on the periphery of their lives, things had to be even better—for Aimee, at least.

Gemma placed a cappuccino in front of her. 'How're you doing?' She dropped into the nearest patient's chair and sipped her latte.

No need to ask what she meant. 'Absolutely fabulous. Aimee's talking non-stop—' about her father '—and loves sleeping in a bed because that means she can get out and come find me whenever it suits her. Dad's fishing regularly for the first time since I got sick and seems to be really enjoying it. But, then, you'd know that.'

Gemma's mouth lifted into a smile.

'Work's humming with more patients than I know what to do with.' She locked eyes with her friend, determined to brazen this out.

'And Charlie? How's she doing?' Gemma stared her down.

Terribly. There didn't seem to be a cure for broken hearts. Being a doctor, she should be able to come up with something to remedy what ailed her but so far that had been a big fail. 'I'm

running between five and six k's a day now.'
And it's boring on my own.

'Still haven't heard from Marshall?'

'Only occasional emails, which tell me next
to nothing about what he's doing.' Twenty-three
days since he'd left. Not that she was counting. 'Aimee will forget who he is soon.' He'd
promised to stay in touch. Foolishly she'd believed that meant regular phone calls or computer video calls, something where Aimee could
see or hear him. Emails didn't cut it with her.

'And Charlie will pretend she's forgotten
him.'

'I miss him so much it hurts physically.' So
much for being strong.

Admitting she loved him hadn't softened the
intensity of her feelings for him or about his
disappearance. If anything, her emotions were
stronger, more focused. As if admitting her love
had painted the world a whole new colour—
glowing golden when he'd been here, dull grey
now he'd gone. 'Unfortunately he's in my head
all the time. There's no let-up. But I can't get
angry at him. I always knew he'd leave and I'd
have to love him from afar.'

Gemma stood up and tossed her empty paper
cup in the bin. 'Give him time. I can't believe
he's gone for good. His love for you and Aimee

came through in everything he did. He might not realise how he feels yet, but he'll get there.'

'You've been reading too many romance stories.' Or talking to Dad. Her despair was obvious even to her. Charlie shrugged. So what? It hurt. Beyond belief. 'Even if he does work that out, he's not giving up his army career for anyone. He doesn't do settled down.' Draining her coffee, she also aimed her paper cup for the bin. It went in. First thing to go right that morning.

Stop feeling sorry for yourself. Get the day started and put all this Marshall stuff aside for a while. Take Aimee swimming at the pool after work.

'Who's your first patient?' Gemma asked, obviously finished with Marshall for a while.

Relieved, Charlie smiled. 'Faye Burnside and her baby. Can you give Ryan his shots after I've seen them?' Smoothing down her skirt, Charlie followed the nurse out to the waiting room.

'Faye, come through. How's your wee man?' She picked up the heavy day bag the young woman had left beside the chair and swung it at her side as she walked to her consulting room. Definitely getting fitter. A few weeks ago she'd have struggled to lift the darned thing.

'Ryan's only waking twice for feeding during the night now. Thank goodness. I thought he'd never get used to sleeping for more than a couple of hours at a time.' Faye sank onto the chair Gemma had recently vacated. 'To think I used to be able to party all night and get up to go to work the next morning.'

'You weren't doing that seven nights a week for weeks on end.'

Charlie smiled as she took Ryan from Faye. 'Hey, gorgeous. You still being a good boy?' Jiggling him in her arms brought memories of Aimee at this age flooding into her mind and whipping up another storm of emotions. The amazing sense of achievement that her body could produce someone so perfect and precious. The instant love, the need to protect. Being a mother was indescribable. Longing for another baby hit hard.

Get over yourself. You're with patients. Not to mention there won't be any more babies. But— No. No more babies. Be happy with the healthy child you have.

Faye interrupted her selfish mental monologue. 'Can you look at Ryan's tummy? Sometimes a bump comes up just below his ribs.'

'Of course. Any other things you're concerned about?' Charlie didn't mind asking new mothers about their worries. Better to clear them up than have mums stressing needlessly. 'I know

I had plenty of questions when Aimee was this little. Being a doctor meant diddly squat.'

Faye grinned as she took Ryan to undress him for Charlie to examine. 'Not at the moment. I have bugged the Plunket nurses with loads of questions. They're so patient, answering everything like I'm not crazy. It was one of them who said I should show you Ryan's tummy.'

'That's what they're there for.' New Zealand's Plunket Society had been around for ever, helping mothers with their newborns.

'There. Do you see that?' Faye gently touched a raised area below her son's ribs.

Charlie carefully palpated the area. 'I think Ryan has a small hernia, which is easily repaired with minor surgery.'

Faye gasped. 'No way. Surgery? But he's so little.'

'Hernias are quite common with infants and the procedure is straightforward.' She'd have been terrified if Aimee had had to have the op done, despite knowing the lack of risk involved.

'Faye, I'll refer you to a surgeon who's excellent with babies. He'll decide if Ryan needs surgery or if he'll take a wait-and-see approach. You really mustn't worry.' Like Faye would take the slightest bit of notice to those words of wisdom. She certainly wouldn't have if this had been Aimee. 'Sorry. Silly thing to say. I'll print out some information for you to take home and read. Show it to your partner, too.'

Faye's face had turned pale as she snapped together the studs down the front of Ryan's romper suit. Lifting him into her arms, she hugged him desperately. 'But he's so happy, doesn't cry like he's in pain or anything.'

'That's because he's not. Sit down for a few minutes. Ask anything that pops into your head.' Charlie answered numerous questions while searching on her computer for medical information and quickly found the relevant notes on infant hernias to print out.

'Here you go. And here's a referral to the surgeon in Rotorua. I'll get Molly to phone through for an appointment while you're here. The sooner Ryan sees him the sooner you can stop worrying.'

'Will we have to wait months for an appointment?' Faye's hand soothed Ryan's back, even though he was the least distressed person in the room.

Shaking her head, Charlie reassured her. 'I imagine you'll see him within a week. Seriously, while this isn't something you wanted to happen, you mustn't get too wound up about it. I bet if you ask at your postnatal group you'll find other mums who've dealt with the same condition and they'll be able to tell you the same as I am. Ryan's going to be fine.'

She escorted Faye to Reception and arranged for Molly to make the appointment. Glancing at the timetable, she turned to the waiting area. 'Beau, come through to the surgical room.'

A twenty-three-year-old man lumbered to his feet, dwarfing everyone around him. 'Sure, Doctor. How are you today?'

Grinning up at him, she replied, 'I'm supposed to ask that.'

'I know.' He grinned back at her. 'How many of these little suckers are you cutting out of me today?'

'Three.'

'Bet you don't let your little girl out in the sun without layers of sun block on.' Beau had a history of basal cell carcinoma. Two had been removed in previous years and now he opted to have anything remotely abnormal removed before it got too big. While non-malignant, the carcinomas would never go away without medical intervention.

'I smother her from top to toe. So much she's probably going to be vitamin D deficient instead.' Hard to get a balance. Too much sun was bad, too little wasn't great either. Just like everything else, steering a middle course often seemed like juggling a bucketful of balls all at once.

Marshall sat in Karen's kitchen, his hands playing with an empty beer bottle. 'Man, it's hot.'

'Hotter than New Zealand?' Karen grinned.

'It was toasty but nothing like this.' He should never have told her about Charlie, but one night two months ago when he'd been to see her after returning from Afghanistan she'd been so down about Rod's death he'd filled in the silences by talking about anything that had come into his head. As Charlie was always in his head, that's who he'd talked about. Today he'd already let slip that he'd flown over to New Zealand to see her.

Karen looked over the rim of her wine glass at him. 'How was Charlie?'

Hot. Sexy. Loving. Wise. And wishing for far too much from him. 'Surprised to see me.' Angry with him, pleased with him, and very disappointed. No surprise there. He'd walked away with a very heavy heart. Now a shaft of jealousy crawled through his gut at the thought of her following through on his stunning piece of advice to find another guy.

'In a good way?' Karen wasn't letting up.

'Yep.' Then the words he'd been holding back, telling the news he'd wanted to share with someone since he'd got back to the States, spewed out. 'We have a daughter. Aimee. Eighteen months old and the cutest little girl I've ever met.' And he missed her as much as her mother. Pulling out his phone, he showed photos of Aimee and Charlie.

Karen's eyes stuck out as if they were on stalks. Her mouth curled into a soft smile. 'Wow, what a little cutie. Got her daddy's eyes.' The smile widened. 'I'm guessing that's Charlie. She's beautiful, too. When do I get to meet them, huh? Are they coming over here?'

'What's this? A quiz show?' Why had he opened his goddamned mouth? Shoving his chair back, he headed for the trash to dump the bottle.

'You bet it is. If Rod was here you'd be spilling the beans to him.' Her voice caught, and twisted his heart at the same time. Her brave face had been all for show.

Spinning around, he crossed to lift her into a gentle hug. 'Take it easy.' With a soft squeeze he sat her back on her chair and circled the table. He wanted that smile back on her face before he left, no matter how fragile it appeared.

'Charlie and Aimee are not coming here. And

I'm not moving to New Zealand. You know how it is with the army sending me all over the show. Hardly fair on Charlie, is it?'

'She said that?' Strength was returning to Karen's voice.

'No. I didn't give her the chance. We're not going down that path. It's too hard on everyone. Imagine how bewildering it would be for a little girl. She'd no sooner start to get to know me than I'd be off again.'

'Better than not knowing you at all.'

'Charlie will find someone else, a guy who can be a regular dad to Aimee.' His gut clenched painfully. Another man raising his kid? Didn't seem right from here. Neither did he feel ecstatic about another guy sharing Charlie's bed. But what was a guy supposed to do if he wanted to protect those he loved?

Karen locked gazes with him. 'I don't believe I'm hearing this. What's happened to you? Leave your brain in Afghanistan? Lose your nerve between battles? Come on, Marshall, you're shirking your duty, never mind your heart.'

'Not fair. You know where my duty lies.' When her eyebrows rose he hurriedly continued before she could say anything else disturbing. 'Charlie lives in the house where she was born. The only time she's left Taupo was to train as a doctor. She works in the same medical centre as her father. Me.' He stabbed his chest with a thumb. 'The longest I've lived in the same place is fifteen months. We are completely incompatible.'

His tongue had got away from him again. It had been happening far too often since he'd returned from New Zealand and that woman who seemed to have stolen his heart and tipped his world upside down.

'Never took you for a scaredy-cat.' Karen gripped his hand. 'I've lost my husband and lover, my kids have lost their father, but we will always remember him and know the love he shared with us. Did you know Rod had decided not to sign up again? He wanted to put us before the army. He believed in us, saw the army had many men, and that we only had him.'

She blinked. 'Marshall, what's staying in the army because of your perceived guilt over his death going to achieve? Nothing. You've got to stop blaming yourself for his death. He wouldn't hold you responsible.'

'He never told me he was getting out.' Rod's timing had sucked. He'd nearly made it. A shiver ran up Marshall's spine. For Rod? Or himself and those he loved? Had he got it all wrong?

Did his men need *him* or would any competent officer suffice? Certainly no one could take his place as father to Aimee, no matter what he'd told Charlie. No man could love Charlie as much as he did. But to walk away from his long-held beliefs, his guilt and start over?

Karen withdrew her hand. 'I'm sorry. You've come visiting, and I appreciate that more than you'll ever know. But I see you missing out on so much. Don't you want to be with someone you love, someone who loves you back so completely you wonder how you survived before you met her?'

Time to get on the road. 'Thanks for lunch, Karen. Call me if there's anything you or the kids need, okay?' He plonked a light kiss on her cheek. 'Say hi to the boys for me.' And he took his leave before she could throw any more off-beat ideas at him.

But her words followed him down the path. To love someone that much? He did love Charlie. That much. It was his love for her that kept him away. He was saving her from heartbreak. But it also hurt that he hadn't been there for her through the most terrible time of her life. He might have a duty to his men but the one to Charlie and Aimee was bigger.

What did he really want out of life? He'd

never made plans for his future past what he did now. Maybe he should be thinking about it.

Back in his motel room he stared at his laptop. Would Charlie mind if he gave her and Aimee an internet call? Why wouldn't she? She'd said she loved him. Suddenly he knew that if Taupo was only a few hours away he'd hop a plane right now, go and see her, hug her small frame to his. But the people he cared about most were at the other end of the world, where they belonged.

And he missed them.

The screen came up and his finger hovered over the internet icon. Click. Click off. Charlie could be at work, or busy bathing Aimee. If he wanted to call her he needed to arrange a time with her.

Her number was on his cellphone. A simple text would sort out that problem.

Charlie came back so quickly he had to wonder if she'd been waiting three weeks to hear from him. Which made him feel bad. She was at home, available any time, but the sooner the better if he wanted to see Aimee.

Click. As he waited for the connection he rummaged through the small fridge for a beer, twisted the top off, gulped a mouthful.

And then they were there, filling his laptop

screen with their smiles and chatter. He stared at Charlie, drinking in the wonderful sight. God, she was beautiful. That crooked smile, those teary eyes filled his heart with tenderness and need.

'Hey.' Aimee's shriek filled the sterile room he stood in with wonder and love and warm fuzzies. Her arms waved at him and her cute face filled the whole screen as she leaned close to the computer. 'Hello, Daddy.'

The beer bottle slid out of his fingers and crashed to the floor. Daddy. As beer spilled across the vinyl he stood transfixed. Daddy. Aimee had called him Daddy for the first time ever. In his chest his heart didn't seem to know what it should be doing. Thumping, squeezing, racing, aching.

'Daddy,' his daughter shouted, her face puckering up at his lack of response.

Swallowing the sudden blockage in his throat, he croaked, 'Hello, Aimee.' Huh? That was it? Your daughter calls you Daddy for the first time and you say, 'Hello Aimee'? What's wrong with you, man?

'Marshall?' The voice of reason washed over him, and Charlie's concerned face slid into the picture next to Aimee's grinning one. 'You okay?'

Of course he wasn't okay. Who would be? Had Charlie set him up? Taught Aimee to use the D word to knock him off his feet? Somehow he didn't think so. She hadn't used dirty tactics before so why would she start now?

Dropping onto a chair, he grunted, 'I'm good. How's everything with you? Not working too hard, I hope.'

Disappointment—or was it annoyance?—altered her voice, made it edgy. 'No more than usual. I took Aimee to the public swimming pool tonight. She's a little seal, flipping all over the place. We can go to the tepid pools when summer's over.' Charlie's face was serious, not at all excited as it usually was when she was talking about Aimee.

He'd done that to her. He swore silently, then gathered his strength. 'Aimee? Can you hear me?'

His daughter's eyes lit up. 'Daddy? Where are you?'

'I'm a long way away, sweetheart.' Too damned far away. Bloody miles and miles. Even if he wanted to kiss her goodnight, he couldn't. 'Did you like swimming in the big pool?'

'Yes, Daddy.' Another ear-piercing shriek.

As Aimee chattered on excitedly he watched every nuance of expression on Charlie's face.

Something was wrong. She blinked too often. Her cheeks were stained red, like she'd been crying. The skin beneath her eyes was swollen.

He wanted to cut across Aimee's chatter to ask what was up but understood he had to wait.

When Aimee finally got bored with talking to the computer she got down and headed away without a backward glance, and he felt a moment of disappointment despite needing to talk to her mother.

Charlie surprised him with, 'There's a chance we might be getting another partner at the centre. A doctor from South Africa has made enquiries and hopes to come and talk to us all next month.'

Marshall sat up straighter.

Charlie continued. 'She seems very keen. Wants to move to a small town rather than a city.'

It was as though a door had slammed in his face. That partnership had been offered to him. Didn't matter that he'd turned it down. 'Brendon will be pleased if she buys in. Give him plenty of time to go fishing then.'

'We'll be eating trout every day of the week.' Her smile didn't override the sadness darkening her eyes.

'Charlie? You're not keen on this South African doctor?'

She shrugged. 'Won't know until I meet her. Sorry, but I've got to put Aimee to bed.' Charlie started to push away from the table her laptop was on.

'Wait. You've been crying. Why?' Why wasn't he there with her? 'Talk to me, babe.'

At first he thought she'd shut down on him but slowly she returned to her chair. 'Keisha's results came back today.'

His blood ran cold. 'That bad?' He pictured that lovely woman who'd come to see Charlie while he'd been there. A person didn't have to be in a war zone for a grenade to be lobbed at them.

Charlie's head dipped. 'Yeah. It's aggressive. The treatment starts very soon and will be tough on her.' Her lips trembled and she began blinking back tears. 'Those poor little boys, Marshall. They need their mum. They're too little to be facing this.'

And Charlie needed someone to hold her, a shoulder to let all the pain out on. Because although she would be hurting for Keisha and her family, Charlie was also reliving her own pain and fear from her own cancer experience, and possibly for the loss of her mother.

'Babe,' he whispered as he put his hand on the screen. 'Put your hand on mine, Charlie. I'm sending my love. You know I love you, right? You can deal with this. We can deal with it. I'm here for you.' Yeah, and he should be *there* for her.

Her eyes met his as her hand touched her screen. 'Thank you.' Her voice shook. 'Maybe I'm not cut out for doctoring in my home town. It's harder than in a hospital where the patients aren't people I went to school with, sailed or cycled with.'

'You do a fabulous job. I bet Keisha would prefer you as her GP right now than anyone else.' He always felt a kinship with the men he treated in the army. He knew them, their families and what they were hoping for.

Just like a GP.

Her smile was wobbly but it was a smile. 'Yeah, you might be right.'

'Of course I'm right.' He grinned. 'Who wants to talk about something as serious as this with a doctor they don't know well?'

'Keisha knows I've been through it so she's asking some hard questions.'

'You've got the answers for her. You won't be saying things that are blatantly untrue.' His grin wavered. He mightn't have been injured in war but he certainly understood the fear of being taken out by a sharpshooter.

He and Charlie weren't that different in their careers. Could he swap location? Change his uniform for an open-necked shirt and slacks? Get weekends off even?

Because he owed Charlie his allegiance more than he owed it to the army. *Thank you, Karen*.

In the background Aimee squealed. Charlie looked disappointed. 'I'd better go. Teddy's spilled his dinner and is in danger of being stuffed into the dishwasher. Can we do this again? Soon?'

'How about tomorrow?' He didn't want her to go. Could have talked to her all night. Tomorrow—a full twenty-four hours away. How could he wait that long?

'Tomorrow's good. I haven't heard anything about what you've been up to yet. Love you.' She blew him a kiss and was gone. Leaving Marshall staring at a photo of Charlie and Aimee on his screen. His heart was heavy. Aimee had called him Daddy. And Charlie was hurting, needed lots of TLC.

Charlie tucked Aimee into bed and kissed her chubby cheeks. 'Goodnight, sweetheart.'

'Where's Daddy? I want him here.'

Her heart clenched so hard it hurt, took her breath away so she couldn't answer immediately. You and me both, her brain screamed. Never once in the last few days when Aimee had learned to say Daddy had Charlie anticipated that question. Aimee was too small to understand much, but it seemed that even she knew her father should be here with her. 'Daddy lives a long way away and can only come to see you when he's not working.'

'Okay, Mummy.' Aimee snuggled down under the light cover, a yawn creasing her face.

'Goodnight, darling.' Another kiss and she crept out of the room, pulling the door closed behind her. Already asking where her father was. What would she be asking by the time she started school?

Pulling on a light jersey, she headed for the kitchen to make a cup of tea before going outside to sit on the veranda in the cooler evening air. The endless clicking sound of cicadas had quieted as the day turned into night. In the distance cars roared along the main road into town. Overhead a plane was on its final approach for the airport. Otherwise the evening was quiet.

So Marshall had called on the internet. Talking to him about Keisha had made her feel better. He seemed to understand her, knew what to say. Damn, she missed him. Would give anything to be able to cuddle up with him.

Dad strolled out and sat on the lounger beside her. 'Progress?'

She couldn't help sighing. 'Who would know? Every day I hoped he'd phone or call me. Every night I've gone to bed angry that he hadn't. Yet now? I should be happy, pleased he got in touch.' The tea was hot on her tongue. 'Yet the more I get, the more I want.'

'Could be you were expecting too much too soon.'

How come Dad always stuck up for the guy? She snapped at him, 'I wasn't hanging out for a proposal.'

'No, love, I'm sure you weren't. But you might've been hoping for more of a connection to his life.' His reasonable tone incensed her, which in turn made her feel terrible. None of this was Dad's fault.

Blinking hard, she strived for a softer tone. 'Marshall made it very clear I'm never going to get that. But I can't stop wishing for it. I love him, Dad.' Where had all these tears come from?

'Even a blind fool could see that.'

'I told him before he left. I don't know what

I thought I'd achieve but it seemed important that he knew.' She set the mug on the boards to cool. 'How can he can ignore that?' Marshall loved her, too. Who or what had hurt him so badly that he truly believed he would be wrong for her and Aimee? Right now, if she had the answer to that, she'd want to strangle that person. Or persons.

'Be patient, Charlotte. Your health's good, and your energy's coming back. Aimee's got you. You wanted to find Marshall so he'd be there for Aimee if anything happened. You've achieved that.'

She'd wanted to find him because she loved him.

Dad added, 'A little over five weeks ago Marshall didn't know he had a child, didn't consider he had other options about how to live his life. He's a man who thinks things through. He doesn't act rashly.'

At least Dad hadn't told her to put it out there and wait to see what happened. She stood up. 'Thanks, Dad, but even I know Marshall is never going to come and live here. I've been fooling myself to even wish he might.'

'You could move to the States.'

'No way. Leave my home, my job? Leave you? Never.' The words shot out of her mouth like bullets. 'No, Dad. No.' Her foot stamped hard on the veranda. 'No.' She'd have preferred putting it out there to this suggestion.

'Just a thought.'

'Not a very good one.' Her dad was the most sensible, grounded person she knew. He didn't have random thoughts. So where had this come from? Did he really believe that her taking his granddaughter to live in another country was a good idea? Or was he being his usual selfless self? Guilt stabbed her. Could it be that he wanted to finally have a life that didn't revolve around looking out for her?

'Dad, you're the best father any girl could wish for. But I can stand on my own two feet now. You need to do some of those things on your dream list.'

She'd even accept the South African doctor if it meant Dad could have a life. The dream of Marshall buying into the medical centre would be over. But she'd still live in this house she'd known all her life, and bring Aimee up as a Kiwi kid at the same schools she'd attended. Insular? Too much so? Was she as afraid of making changes as Marshall? Perhaps she was. That needed some thought.

Unfortunately Dad hadn't finished. 'America is only twelve hours away by plane.'

'Drop it, Dad.'

But later, lying in bed, she couldn't let the crazy idea go. Why not move to another country? She'd enjoyed her time in Hawaii. That had been for a few months. Not a lifetime. It was hard to imagine living somewhere else and making plans for the future that didn't involve her home town. How could she walk away from people she'd known all her life? But Marshall would be there for her, with her. Some of the time anyway. He'd be a part of those plans. He could share raising Aimee, really be a part of her life, instead of dropping in occasionally via the internet.

Charlie held up a finger in front of her face. She loved Marshall with all her heart. He was the only man she ever wanted to be with.

A second finger went up. Marshall was Aimee's dad. They should be together.

The third finger. Marshall loved her.

Fourth point. She could be a doctor anywhere. There'd be some legalities, but nothing insurmountable.

Fifth point. There wasn't one. Definitely not a positive one.

Could she move away from all she knew for the man she loved?

Her fingers folded into a fist and her hand dropped to her tummy. Marshall would never agree to this madcap idea anyway.

CHAPTER TWELVE

MARSHALL PULLED THE SUV over to the kerb on the left and hauled on the handbrake. At least he'd made it without any incidents involving other vehicles. Glancing further along the road, he grinned to see John's newly panel-beaten and painted work vehicle parked in the same spot it had been the day he'd pranged it.

'Bet if John knew I might breeze by he'd have parked it in his driveway.'

Using his shoulder to shove the door open, he climbed out to stand, hands on hips, staring around him. His heart hammered against his ribs. His mouth dried while his eyes moistened. There hadn't been a night since he'd left he hadn't thought of this place. If he'd been a romantic kind of guy he'd have said he'd left his heart in Taupo that day. Not anywhere in Taupo but right at this address, this house that begged to be filled with kids and laughter, with happy adults and fun times around the barbecue with friends.

Looking over at the house Charlie had grown up in, he noted the windows and front door weren't wide open as they had been in January. April here was cooler. Driving down from Auckland he'd noted that the trees were beginning to change colour as autumn sent out its first chilly tentacles. Though not the trees in Charlie's yard. They were evergreens. Solid native trees the likes of which he'd never seen before coming here.

The paddling pool had disappeared. No one sat on the veranda, though the lounger still remained in its place. Charlie must be inside because her car was parked on the other side of the closed gate. He didn't know if he was pleased or disappointed she wasn't in the same place she'd been that first day he'd turned up.

He'd come to talk to her, to tell her his plans for the future. So why was he suddenly shaking? He was doing the right thing. He was doing what he wanted, needed to do. Until now he'd believed Charlie might be pleased with his decision. Yet standing on the road outside her house, he felt an alien fear. What if she'd decided she was better off without him? Worse, could she have already met another man?

No. She'd told him she loved him. Charlie wouldn't be replacing him that easily or quickly. From what he'd seen of her and Aimee and Brendon, love in the Lang family was for ever. He just had to expand his horizons and allow this family into his heart.

Too late, mate. They're already there. Which is why you're taking this enormous risk.

That, and because life wasn't worth much without these people in it.

'Daddy.' The sweetest young voice on the planet shrieked from somewhere behind the fence. His stomach crunched, his heart played a weird tattoo against his ribs. And his mouth lifted from grim to happy. He stepped across the road.

Another shriek, louder still. 'Daddy's here. Lift me up.'

From the flowerbed where she was planting daffodil bulbs Charlie jerked back on her heels so fast her neck cricked. 'Aimee?' She couldn't have seen Marshall. He was in Kansas. 'Aimee, come here.' Away from strangers. Away from the disappointment that was sure to follow when she realised that her daddy had not suddenly appeared.

Ever since the day she'd called Marshall Daddy

as they'd talked on the computer Aimee had been talking about Daddy, looking for him in cupboards and under beds. It had broken Charlie's heart to see the tears well up every time Aimee came to her and said, 'Daddy's gone away.'

She looked around the empty lawn. 'Aimee, where are you?'

'Hello, Charlie.'

Her heart stopped. 'Marshall?' she squeaked. That deep, velvety voice sounded like his. Her gaze lifted slowly, fearful of finding a stranger looking down at her. The thighs filling out those tight jeans seemed familiar, the narrow hips, the broad chest stretching a light woollen jersey. She swallowed hard. And lifted her chin enough to see the face belonging to this body. Green eyes glittered down at her, a hesitant smile caught at her, and a hand reached down for hers.

'Marshall?' she whispered, as she placed her soil-stained hand into that firm grasp.

With a gentle tug from Marshall she stood upright, balancing precariously on her toes, drinking in the sight before her. Words had deserted her. Her world was tipping all over the place. The only vision filling her hungry eyes was the man who'd owned her head space for weeks. Could this be a mirage? The hand holding hers felt real; solid, strong, warm, right. The eyes holding a steady gaze were real. The arm gripping Aimee like he'd never, ever let her go was real.

'Marshall.' Her voice came out low and quiet. 'You came.' But for how long?

'Couldn't stay away another moment.' His smile slipped. 'I'm sorry it took so long for the truth to hit me. I really believed I could walk away and let you get on with finding a better life. How dumb was that?'

'About as dumb as me thinking I could let you go without putting up a fight.'

His free arm went around her shoulders, pulling her close to him. 'I've missed you both. You have no idea how much.'

Oh, yes, she did, but who was she to argue? She'd been going crazy with the need to see him. 'I have to kiss you to know I'm not dreaming.'

'Can't argue with that.' As his head came down closer and closer to hers a familiar tension wound through her, a hot tautness that had everything to do with recognition. Her body knew this man. A kiss wasn't going to change a thing. But, still, a girl had to kiss her man when he came home, didn't she?

Then Marshall pulled back. His steady gaze

locked with hers. 'This is for ever, Charlie. I've left the army, packed up my few belongings and shipped them out here. I've even made enquiries about registering with the New Zealand Medical Council.'

Her tongue stuck to the roof of her mouth, preventing her saying anything, so she nodded, waiting for him to go on.

'It isn't going to be easy. I've never stopped in one place long enough to see two Christmases in a row. I don't know what it's like to treat the same patients month in, month out, to become involved with them and their families.' He sucked in air. 'And I certainly have no idea about living in a loving family. But I want to give it my absolute best shot.'

'Then it will work out just fine.'

'You know I love you, don't you?' A hint of uncertainty underscored his question.

Tapping her chest, she smiled. 'Right in here I feel your love all the time.' Reaching up on tiptoe again, she said against his mouth, 'And now for that kiss.'

His lips brushed hers and then he pulled back again. 'One more thing.' This was getting to be an annoying habit of his.

She gave him a mock glare. 'This had better

be good, Marshall Hunter. A girl can only wait so long for a kiss.'

His mouth twitched like he was holding in a laugh. 'You'll get all the kisses you want once you answer my next question.' Juggling Aimee on his hip, he used his other hand to brush a strand of hair off her cheek. 'Charlotte Lang, will you marry me, be my lifelong partner and keep me grounded? Share the raising of our daughter with me?'

Doubt suddenly rose in her, dwarfing the hope in her heart. 'What about having more children?' His frown creased his forehead and when his mouth opened to answer her she raced on. 'I can't have any more babies. Ever. Have you thought about that?'

The frown disappeared, and his gorgeous mouth curved into a sensational, toe-curling smile. 'Babe, you and Aimee are all I need. You'll both be running rings around me as it is. I don't need any other children to make me happy. I've already got everything I could ever want.'

For the life of her she couldn't move. Her legs had turned all jellylike and her body felt weightless. Warmth flowed through her, touching every corner, knocking out the chills. Marshall wanted her, wanted to be with her, for ever.

'In case your hearing has got bad these past

weeks, I'll repeat myself. Charlie Lang, will you do me the honour of marrying me?'

Whipping her hand out from his fingers, she gripped his arm and held on. Marry Marshall? 'Yes, yes, yes, and yes.' He had asked four things of her, hadn't he? 'Yes, Marshall, my love and my lover and the father of my child, I will become Mrs Charlie Hunter.' Stretching up, she begged, 'Now can I have that kiss?'

Some kisses were made in heaven. This one had been brewing since the day they'd met in the ED in Honolulu, and had only just reached its full potential. It had the right blend of love and desire and commitment and dedication. It spoke of their future—together. It was all about love.

* * * * *